"It C_____"

"Why not? There's lots of evidence that they were real."

"Legends aren't evidence," he informed her dryly. "Scientifically there's no basis for the assumption that this is anything other than . . ."

"Than what?" she prodded.

"I'm not sure yet. I do know what it isn't."

"What do you call that then?" pointing at the horn beside his foot.

"Keratin."

"In English, Adam. And you know that whatever it was you said wasn't what I meant."

"Same stuff as fingernails," he said, still avoiding committing himself.

"You are in the process of evading my question," she reminded him.

"I wasn't trying to avoid an answer. It's just that right now I don't have one. I'm certain there's a reasonable explanation for all of this."

"Meaning you refuse to admit that it *could* be a unicorn."

Dear Reader,

Welcome to Silhouette! Our goal is to give you hours of unbeatable reading pleasure, and we hope you'll enjoy each month's six new Silhouette Desires. These sensual, provocative love stories are both believable and compelling—sometimes they're poignant, sometimes humorous, but always enjoyable.

Indulge yourself. Experience all the passion and excitement of falling in love along with our heroine as she meets the irresistible man of her dreams and together they overcome all obstacles in the path to a happy ending.

If this is your first Desire, I hope it'll be the first of many. If you're already a Silhouette Desire reader, thanks for your support! Look for some of your favorite authors in the coming months: Stephanie James, Diana Palmer, Dixie Browning, Ann Major and Doreen Owens Malek, to name just a few.

Happy reading!

Isabel Swift
Senior Editor

SDRL-7/85

CHRISTINE FLYNN
The Myth and the Magic

Silhouette Desire

Published by Silhouette Books New York

America's Publisher of Contemporary Romance

SILHOUETTE BOOKS
300 East 42nd St., New York, N.Y. 10017

Copyright © 1986 by Christine Flynn

ISBN: 0-373-05296-0

First Silhouette Books printing August 1986

America's Publisher of Contemporary Romance

Printed in the U.S.A.

CHRISTINE FLYNN

admits to two obsessions: reading and writing, and three "serious" preoccupations: gourmet cooking, her family (she has a daughter and a husband she unabashedly describes as the sexiest best friend a girl could ever have) and travel. She tried everything from racing cars to modelling before settling into what she loves best—turning her daydreams into romance novels.

One

You found a *what*?" Stephanie choked back a disbelieving laugh as she followed J.J. Johnson toward the gaping pit now comprising half of her backyard. Three men—two squatting, one standing—were gathered in the far end of that hole. "In there?"

No sooner had Stephanie pulled her battered old MG into the garage and dumped her suitcase and the wallpaper-sample book she'd borrowed from her dad on the kitchen floor, than the contractor she'd hired to put in her pool had started pounding on the back door. She still couldn't believe what she'd heard him say. From the look on his weathered face, he was having trouble believing it himself—even though it had been his backhoe that had uncovered the skeleton he'd just tentatively identified.

The skeleton. Despite the humid June heat, an icy shiver skittered along her spine. The thought of anything other than tulip bulbs being buried in her back-yard gave her the creeps.

"Well," the contractor drawled, his voice taking on a low, conspiratorial note when he stopped her several feet from the deep hole. "The forensics guy from the police department didn't exactly say it was a dinosaur. He just said the bone he took back with him Friday wasn't human. That's why I had my boys come back this morning. I thought we could finish the excavating, but then this other fella showed up about the same time we did, and he seems to think it's one of those extinct things like they find over at the tar pits and that sorta goes along with what the other guy was saying."

It was too much too fast, and Stephanie still wasn't sure she was understanding what she was hearing. Though she had no idea why they were using it, she spoke in the same hushed tone he had. "Mr. Johnson, let's take this one thing at a time. First, you called the police?"

His shoulders lifted with a shrug. "Had to. Anytime a contractor runs across something that looks like it might've been human, he's got to notify the police. Can lose your license if you don't."

"I see," she returned, refusing to dwell on the unsavory circumstances that made that particular requirement necessary. "But since you know it isn't anything the police are interested in, can't you just get rid of it?"

With one hand clamped over the back of his thick neck, he shook his head. "It's not that easy, ma'am. According to what I was told a while ago, the police department notified some state historic office, and they contacted the guy down in the hole now that thinks it's a dinosaur."

The only response appropriate for that convoluted explanation seemed to be a slightly baffled "Oh-kay." She wasn't at all certain that her comprehension of the situation was any better now than it had been fifteen seconds ago. She thought he'd said it was the man from the police department who thought it was...

Oh, forget it, she mentally muttered and aimed for the heart of the matter. "So now what do we do?"

"That's just it. I know you were expecting most of this to be done by the time you got back—" tipping back the brim of his baseball cap, he nodded in the general direction of his idle crew "—but until that Dr. Colter down there decides who's going to dig it out, we can't do any more work."

The midmorning sun shone brightly over the tiled roof of Stephanie's small, beige stucco house. Shielding her dark gray eyes from the glare, she muttered, "Wonderful," and ran her fingers through the knots the wind had tied in her shoulder-length, caramel-colored hair. One of these days she'd remember to wear a scarf when she drove her car with the top down. Better yet, she'd get the top fixed so she could put it up.

The frown that had replaced her usual easy smile deepened when she turned around and glanced at the man occupying the space between the two capable-looking youths J.J. called his "boys." That had to be Dr. Colter. Her attention, though, wasn't on who he was, so much as on the maroon shirt he was wearing. That shirt covered a very broad set of shoulders, and the way its owner was crouched to poke at the dirt caused his light khaki slacks to stretch snugly over a nice, tight little...

Giving her head a shake—and telling herself the only reason she was paying any attention at all to some stranger's backside was because it provided a barrier preventing her from seeing what the men were so interested in—she ventured forward another step. Visions of a mammoth skeleton, something on the scale of a *Tyrannosaurus Rex*, kept popping into her head.

A monster on a decidedly smaller scale came scampering over the mound of dirt she was standing on and charged across the yard. J.J. had been so insistent that she come outside immediately that she'd forgotten to close the back door. "Zeus!" she hollered after the tiny dog. "Come back here!"

Three pairs of male eyes jerked up, but Stephanie's were on the black ball of fluff tumbling head over paw down to the "shallow end" of the pool. She wasn't afraid he'd hurt himself. She just didn't want him doing anything embarrassing to one of the men gaping up at her.

Zeus rolled to his feet and in a split second had disappeared into a forest of male legs.

"Hey! Come back here with that!"

Shouting with the savagery of Apollo chasing Python into its cave, the guy with the nice...shoulders scrambled up the side of the hole after nine pounds of pure holy terrier. Zeus had something that looked like a dirt-caked stick almost as long as he was clamped firmly in his little jaws and was making considerably better progress up the embankment than his pursuer.

"Bring that back here, you damn little mutt!"

The man looked furious, and his tone matched his expression perfectly. Stephanie didn't see his face, though, she was too busy seeing red. How dare he call her precious puppy a damn little mutt! Only she could call him that.

"He won't stop if you keep chasing him," she shot back, oblivious to the amused grins creasing the workers' faces. "Stop yelling at him."

The man followed the lightning-quick streak of black behind one of the bougainvillea-covered posts supporting the patio roof. The dog slipped through the heavily bracketed limbs, skirted a terra-cotta pot holding a wilted geranium and came running toward her, his little head tilted up to balance the awkward weight of his prize.

A deep, feral growl—this one of the human variety—came from behind the bush. "Somebody get that away from him. He's got part of a rib!"

"I don't care if he's got the crown jewels," she retorted, heading Zeus off as he plunged under a chair by the patio table. "He won't give anything up if you run after him. He thinks you're playing." Her voice softened to a placating coo when she squatted down beside the white iron chair. "Come on, punkin," she coached. "Give me that nasty old bone."

For a moment Zeus just stood under the seat looking blankly up at his mistress. Black lashes slowly blinked, then, giving the bone a tug, he deposited it beside Stephanie's sandaled foot. She wasn't about to pick it up.

"Good boy," she soothed as a pair of feet considerably larger than her own appeared on the grass edging the concrete patio.

From her position about a foot and a half away, she saw a fine layer of dust covering a pair of comfortably worn loafers. The right loafer stepped forward, a large hand claimed the ten-inch scrap of bone, then both the hand and the feet disappeared. A moment later, those dusty shoes were back.

Still running her hand over Zeus's soft fur, she edged a cautious glance from the cuffs to the knees of a pair of khakis. It didn't take any great powers of deduction to figure out who they belonged to. The other three men in the yard were all wearing jeans.

Lifting her head, she allowed herself to focus on the little green alligator on the pocket of his maroon knit shirt. A few wisps of gold-colored hair peeked from his open collar, and a very determined jawline was visibly clenched.

Her eyes didn't want to move from that jaw. Somewhere in the back of her mind she knew what she'd see when she finally met his eyes. Being a basically peaceable person, she wanted to postpone that collision as long as possible. Intuition told her that irritation would be the least she'd find.

The Fates really seemed to have it in for her today. First, she'd planned on leaving San Diego at five o'clock this morning—she'd spent the first week of her summer vacation visiting her parents there—but her mother had insisted that she eat breakfast before she left. That delay had put her an hour behind schedule and right in the middle of the Monday-morning traffic on the Santa Ana freeway. A drive that should only have taken two hours had taken three and a half. Then, the box Zeus had been chewing on in the front seat hadn't been the one containing his dog biscuits after all and, except for what the wind had blown out, there was powdered grout all over the inside of her car. Now there was the present matter whose outcome had yet to be determined.

With resignation, she forced her glance past his compressed lips—and sucked in a quiet, stabilizing breath.

What she saw would have rocked her to her toes had there been any feeling left in her legs. Her squatting position had cut off her circulation, and the needlelike prickles in her feet left no room for other sensations. Impressions, however, were another matter. Only moments ago, she'd compared his rantings to those of a thundering god. That analogy had been more accurate than she'd realized.

The man was Apollo. Well, not literally, of course. But he did bear a startling resemblance to the picture gracing the textbook she'd bought for the mythology class she was going to take. Everything about the man—from the deep, stormy blue of his eyes and shades of pale blond threading his thick and slightly curly hair to the leashed power revealed in his rigid stance—reminded her of that fabled Greek god. All he needed was a tunic of golden panther skin draped over that gorgeous body and a quiver of arrows to clench in his fist and the picture would be frighteningly complete. She could only hope that this Dr. Colter person wasn't quite as rash as the gods when he was angry.

And he did look angry. At least he had just a moment ago. Now, his expression, like hers, had gone blank. But those eyes. What remained there was a strange, almost tangible intensity that seemed to pull at her midsection and make it impossible for her to do anything other than stare up at him. It looked like he'd been about to say something, but for a few rather unnerving seconds he couldn't seem to do anything but look at her, either.

His gaze slowly lowered to the vee of her pink T-shirt, lingering on the view his superior position allowed, then rested briefly on the long legs emerging from the hem of her white shorts. All traces of that decidedly male, and very mortal, inspection vanished when he deigned to meet her eyes again. "I would very much appreciate it," he said tightly, "if you'd keep that overgrown rat away from the excavation."

Stephanie was a reasonable person, and reason told her she didn't have to stay here and take orders from this bad-tempered and alarmingly attractive stranger. "That overgrown rat," she replied, pulling her five feet four inches up to its full, unimposing height, "happens to live here. Since it's my yard, he can go anywhere he wants."

Zeus had always been a rather bright, not to mention perverse, puppy. When Stephanie looked down at him, he *was* going where he wanted—on the lawn, inches away from the man's foot.

Either Apollo, er, Dr. Colter, she mentally corrected, didn't notice, or he was choosing to ignore the blatant display of canine ownership. Eyeing her through the narrowed bank of his heavy brown lashes, he nodded toward the hole. "This may be your property, but the remains in there are in the public domain and belong to the state of California. The law provides for the preservation of archaeological and paleontological finds, and I believe what your contractor uncovered falls within the scope of those provisions."

Oh, good grief, she groaned to herself, mimicking his superior position by planting her hands on her hips. "I'm not going to argue with you about who owns what and, law or no law, you're welcome to whatever's in that hole. I certainly don't want it. All I want is to know how long it's going to take to get whatever it is out of there so they can finish putting in my pool."

He seemed to hesitate. Stephanie didn't know if he was estimating how long the work would take or just trying to calm himself down. Maybe he, too, realized it was probably the gathering heat as much as anything else that was causing two strangers to act like twelve-year-olds.

"Ordinarily," he finally said, "it would only take a few days."

"Ordinarily? This isn't ordinarily?"

Rubbing his fingers along his beautifully molded jaw, he looked first at the hole, then back at her. A smile that was somewhere between apologetic and downright sexy pulled at his mouth. "Not quite. Before we get to that, though, I think it best that we start this all over. I'm Adam Colter," he said, and extended his hand. "Paleontologist from UCLA. If you own this place, you must be Mrs. Moore."

"Miss or Ms.," she corrected automatically.

"You're not married?"

She shook her head. "No."

"Well, that should make things a little easier."

Where did that glint in his eyes come from? Was it interest? The sun? "I beg your pardon?"

"Had there been a Mr. Moore," he explained easily, "I'd need to talk with him, too. This way I only have to explain things once."

Obviously just the sun, she told herself, feeling a flicker of feminine disappointment. Then she blinked at her hand. She didn't remember accepting his, but somehow her fingers had disappeared inside his firm grip. He didn't seem to be in any hurry to let go, and judging from the way he was watching her, he didn't seem to mind the fact that she wasn't making any attempt to release his hand. Maybe she'd better start concentrating on what she was doing instead of on the dimple his smile had exposed.

Taking a step back, she pushed her hands into her pockets. "Dr. Colter," she began, wishing he'd stop smiling so that dimple would go away. It was terribly distracting. *He* was terribly distracting. "You started to say something about this not being ordinary. I couldn't agree with you more, but you're obviously referring to something other than the fact that I seem to have a skeleton in my backyard."

"I don't know that it's a complete skeleton yet," he clarified, and arched a wing of thick, golden brown eyebrow. "Would you like to see what we do have?"

"No."

"All you can see right now is the part of the rib cage the backhoe sliced through and a small section of..."

Oh, please, she groaned to herself, and cut him off before his description could become more graphic. "I'd really rather not."

Wondering if the tan she'd been working on all week was doing anything to hide an almost certain pallor, she met his eyes as evenly as she could. He didn't look like this was bothering him at all. If anything, he just seemed a little puzzled by her less-than-enthusiastic response to his offer. "Would you please just tell me who's going to get rid of it, and when?"

"I'd sorta be interested in knowin'' that myself, sir." J. J. Johnson wiped the perspiration from his brow with the back of his forearm. "If it isn't something me and the boys can take out, and if it's going to take you longer than a day or so, I'm afraid I'll have to put the lady's pool at the end of the list. I was sort of squeezing this one in as a favor, and I've got other contracts waiting."

The roar of the backhoe being fired up caused Dr. Colter to withhold an immediate reply. J.J.'s boys were backing it through the section of fence they'd removed earlier, apparently having anticipated that their work was finished here for a while.

Stephanie turned to the shorter of the two men beside her. J.J. was the father of a student she'd worked with at the local high school, where she was employed as a guidance counselor. Last fall, when she'd convinced his sixteen-year-old son to stay in school, the grateful father had offered to put a pool in for her at cost.

For Stephanie, the fact that the boy would be continuing his education was thanks enough. She hated the thought of someone all but condemning their future at such an early age. But a pool was something she'd considered ever since she'd bought her house two years ago. With Mr. Johnson's kind offer, along with the money she'd originally saved to go to Greece, she was now acquiring one. Or trying to.

"The end of your list?" she asked as the noise from the backhoe faded off.

There was a genuine regret in J.J.'s expression. "It'll be three, maybe four weeks before I can get back here. The excavation should've been done by now and the rebar almost in so we could blow in the cement. I'm real sorry, ma'am. We'd'a been on schedule if we hadn't run into that thing."

J.J. and Stephanie turned to Dr. Colter, who was beginning to look a little defensive. Not surprising since he was looking down at expressions that seemed to be accusing him of putting the obstacle in the hole himself.

"At the very least, it'll take a couple of weeks," he informed the stocky contractor, and Stephanie frowned at the odd, placating note edging into his voice. "A professional crew has to be brought in and since we don't know how extensive the find is, it's really impossible to give you a definite amount of time. If the remains are intact, it won't take anywhere near as long to remove them as it will if they were scavenged and scattered. If they are scattered, we'll need to do more extensive excavation."

Though Stephanie had moved a couple of feet away, she was still listening to every word being said. Zeus had laid claim to one of the workers' gloves and she wanted to get it away from him before he could chew a hole through the finger. Scooping the puppy into her arms, she handed the glove to J.J. with an apologetic smile and looked up at Adam.

"Then, there's something I'd like to ask you," he was saying. He cast a wary eye at Zeus curled quite comfortably against Stephanie's breast before raising his eyes to hers. "Which could make the dig take longer. What I want to ask is a little extraordinary, but I'd appreciate it if you'd hear me out before you say no."

A half an hour later, Stephanie was shaking her head while she watched the racy red Porsche pull away from the curb in front of her house. Being the person she was, she'd quietly informed Dr. Adam "Apollo" Colter that she was hardly in the habit of answering a question before it had been asked, then carefully listening to everything he had to say—only about half of which she'd understood. Mitigating fossilized remains was an area she knew absolutely nothing about. It looked like that was about to change, however.

Turning away from the picture window in her soon-to-be-repainted living room, she headed through the kitchen and out into the garage to unload the tiles from the trunk of her car. She'd purchased the tiles, along with several gallons of paint, from her parents' hardware store, and was feeling pretty good about the money she was saving by doing the remodeling work herself. The "daughter's discount" her dad had given her hadn't hurt much, either. She just wished she could feel as happy about the answer she'd given Dr. Colter.

What he had asked of her was reasonable enough she supposed, under the circumstances. And since the contractor was going to be delayed anyway, it wasn't like the whole thing would be a terrible inconvenience—except for having to keep Zeus and maybe some curious onlookers out of the backyard every day.

All of that sounded terribly logical for an admittedly illogical person. But that wasn't what bothered her. What concerned her was that the intuition she always relied on—and which seldom failed her—had taken an ill-timed leave of absence. One minute it had been telling her she was asking for trouble if she went along with what he wanted, and the next, she wasn't paying any attention to anything but that darn dimple of his. Instead of politely refusing his request and preserving what remained of her plans for the summer, she'd muttered something terribly decisive like, "I guess it'd be all right," then had to remind herself to breathe when he'd added that debilitating smile to his thanks.

She really wasn't sure why she'd said yes.

Neither was Adam, and he still couldn't believe his luck. Not that he ever put stock in something so illogical as mere instinct, but after the way he'd acted when that dog of hers had run off with that precious piece of bone, he'd been sure she'd say no.

Pulling up to a stop sign in the quiet residential neighborhood not far from the UCLA campus, he glanced at the specimen on the seat. The bone fragment the police lab had sent over to the university hadn't been dated yet, but Adam recognized a fossil when he saw one. Now, having seen the site himself, he'd confirmed his first suspicions. The soil where it had been found was heavy with the sediment of oil and asphalt that had preserved it. Since the site was only a few miles from the La Brea Tar Pits, the thing in Stephanie Moore's pool—or what would eventually be her pool—was probably a mammal like those found there. Nothing earth-shattering in the world of scientific discovery, but exciting to him nonetheless. Exciting because it provided an opportunity he wouldn't have had otherwise. Thanks to Ms. Moore, his summer-term class on vertebrate paleontology didn't have to share a dig site with everybody else at the tar pits. For the next few weeks, his lab would be in that very intriguing lady's backyard.

The first thing he'd noticed when the small, slender woman had glanced up from her protective position by her puppy was that she was older than she'd first appeared. He'd barely glanced at her while they'd been chasing after the dog, and with those high, firm breasts and the lithe legs of a runner, he'd expected her to be a teenager. The daughter of the people who owned the property, perhaps. Then that tangle of shining, terribly disheveled honey-brown hair had been pushed back to reveal a finely boned face and eyes the color of midnight.

It was the awareness he'd seen so briefly in those haunting gray-black eyes, and the tiny little lines furrowing their corners when they narrowed, that made him realize she was only a few years younger than his own thirty-three. For some reason he still couldn't understand, the way she'd looked up at him had had a very unsettling impact. Maybe that was why he'd come off sounding like a pompous bureaucrat when he started spouting that stuff about state law and preservation rights.

He almost groaned out loud at that thought. Nice way to make an impression. Not that it matter_1. He thought he'd been pretty skillful in finding out her marital status, but she hadn't done a thing—subtly or otherwise—to find out about his. Obviously she wasn't interested.

The sharp honk behind him shook Adam from those vaguely dissatisfying thoughts. He had no business thinking about her right now anyway. After he stopped by his office on campus, he'd have less than an hour to get to his apartment, change clothes and pick up Barbara for their tennis date. No, that wasn't quite right. Diane was tennis. Barbara was lectures and the theater. It wouldn't do at all to show up for the symposium on The Prognostication of the Evolutionary Chain wearing tennis whites. Barbara was a stickler for those kinds of things.

Instead of his mind's eye conjuring up a picture of the coolly aloof Professor Barbara Wainwright, the only image that formed was of a woman he didn't even know. A woman who probably hadn't even known she was smiling when she'd cuddled her tiny dog against the gentle roundness beneath her soft pink T-shirt.

He didn't even like pink.

Two

"Stephanie? Where are you?"

Pulling herself to her knees, Stephanie peered over the counter separating her small U-shaped kitchen from her breakfast nook. A head of bright strawberry-blond curls had poked itself inside her back door.

"I'm right here, Linda." With the roll of masking tape she was holding, she waved her next-door neighbor into the kitchen. "What's up?"

"That's what I wanted to ask you. By the way, welcome home."

Stephanie smiled. "Thanks."

"Well? What's going on?"

"I'm taping off the baseboards so I can start painting."

"Not that." Linda leaned her reed-thin frame against the door to close it and picked up the puppy wriggling at her feet. Linda's terrier was Zeus's mother, so each owner considered the other's pet "family." "I mean back there. You can't believe the traffic that's been in and out of your yard since Friday. There was even a cop here, for God's sake, and Eleanor Dobbs.... Well, you know Eleanor. She was over here the second she saw the police car, then came pounding on my door to tell me that some poor soul had met its demise in your backyard. She was so excited I thought her pacemaker'd short out for sure."

Eleanor's reaction wasn't particularly surprising. The woman was the neighborhood busybody, and those who knew her had a tendency to largely ignore both the woman and her gossip. Stephanie had the dubious honor of living right across the street from her.

A wry little smile pulled at Stephanie's lips as she rounded the counter and handed Linda one of the two diet colas she took from the refrigerator. "This might take a while," she explained, nodding toward the white rattan chairs surrounding the glass-topped table. She'd already put the peach-and-cream place mats that matched her new color scheme on it, though the walls were still the same bland white they'd always been. By tomorrow night she hoped that the kitchen would be a soft tint of pale peach. She'd finished the breakfast nook as soon as she found the right wallpaper. "How long have you got?"

Tossing a green tennis ball from one of the chairs, Linda settled Zeus in her lap and checked her watch. "The boys are at softball practice. Don't have to pick them up for about an hour."

Satisfied that the allotted time would be adequate, Stephanie cryptically announced, "You're not going to believe this," and proceeded to prove that prediction.

"You're right," Linda confirmed somewhat later. "I don't believe it. Not the part about the fossil...I guess those things can turn up just about anywhere. What I don't believe is that you didn't just tell the guy that if he wanted that thing, he'd have to get it out of there pronto. Obviously your contractor will have to be delayed for a while, but even if he can't get back to it until the middle of July, you'd at least have your pool by the first of August. This way, I'll bet he won't even be able to start on it until then. If you're lucky, you'll be able to begin using it about the time you're due back at school."

"It's only a pool," Stephanie muttered in defense of herself, only to have Linda hit with bigger artillery.

"Then, there's the details to consider . . . like whose bathroom all those people are going to use and whose refrigerator they'll want to stash their lunches in."

Despite the frown lining Stephanie's forehead, she was actually welcoming Linda's practicality. All the rationalization she'd done about the wisdom of granting Adam Colter's request had been completed after the fact. Listening to Linda was helping put the situation into a perspective she'd missed before. From this particular angle, the whole thing was suddenly sounding like a monumental imposition.

Linda wasn't supposed to change tactics and agree with her. But she did. "Your attitude is certainly more admirable than mine would be under these circumstances. I suppose doing your kind of work made you consider the educational opportunity you'd provide by letting a bunch of college kids trample through your backyard. Being in real estate doesn't exactly breed patience with delays, you know . . . though God knows there's plenty of them."

Linda wasn't a real estate agent herself; Ed, her husband, was. Linda, however, sweated out every sale with him and considered her part of the job just as important as his. One of the things Stephanie admired about the arrangement was Ed's conviction that his wife's moral support an absolute necessity.

"So," Linda continued, casting an inquisitive glance out the window behind her, "what're you going to do while the nutty professor and his crew are doing whatever it is they're going to do?"

Stephanie started to say that her plans for the remaining two and a half months of her vacation were still pretty much the same. Linda's remark stopped her. "What makes you call him the 'nutty professor'?"

Absently petting the ball of fur licking her knee, Linda shrugged. "Preconceived notions, I guess. You didn't say anything about the man personally, but someone who teaches... What did you say? Archaeology?"

"Paleontology. There's a difference. According to what I was told this morning, archaeologists study things like artifacts and dwellings. Paleontologists study things that lived."

"Whatever. They both sound dull. Anyway, I'd picture a man who teaches something like that as balding and... No. He's got thinning hair, wears horn-rimmed glasses, mismatched socks and wrinkled shirts, and I'll bet he mutters to himself a lot. Right?"

Linda's smile was infectious, and her stereotyped description caused Stephanie's own grin to widen. Dr. Colter had definitely muttered, but Linda hadn't even come close with the rest of her speculation.

A few details had been omitted from Stephanie's recount of the morning's events—every one of which had to do with the man she'd mentioned only as Dr. Colter. Maybe it was because she was feeling a little silly about the comparison she'd drawn between him and the mythical Apollo. Or perhaps it was because every time she thought about the way he'd looked at her, she got that inexplicable tightening in her stomach again. The sensation wasn't unpleasant. Just unfamiliar, and a little disturbing.

"Well, you got one out of five," she informed her friend. "Let's just say he's . . . interesting."

Linda had been about to take a sip of her cola. Instead, she lowered the can to the table and knitted her coppery eyebrows together. It was the same look she bestowed on her seven- and nine-year-old sons whenever they got into something they weren't supposed to. Stephanie had often thought that expression quite effective and had used it on a few of her students—with very satisfactory results.

"There's something you're not telling me," Linda accused. "Balding men who wear glasses and wrinkled shirts aren't 'interesting.' "

"I didn't say he was bald. You did."

"Stephanie. Don't make this difficult. You know I'll eventually find out what's going on, so why don't you save me the trouble of having to nag it out of you and explain why you're grinning like that."

Stephanie didn't even realize she was grinning. Unable to manage complete sobriety, she turned her smile to the puppy on Linda's lap. "Okay, so I understated it a little. He is intriguing, though." The curve of her lips lowered perceptibly. "And pushy, short-tempered and irritating." When Linda didn't appear convinced that those qualities constituted "interesting," Stephanie calmly added, "He also happens to be gorgeous."

For about two seconds Linda just stared across the table. Then she complacently declared, "That explains it."

Knowing exactly what her friend was alluding to, Stephanie quickly sought to disabuse her of that thought. "It doesn't explain anything. That thing has to be dug

out one way or the other and my decision to let him hold
his class out there had nothing to do with his dimple. I
don't even know if he's married. Just because he wasn't
wearing a ring doesn't mean anything."

To her surprise Linda overlooked her reference to the
dimple she hadn't meant to mention. "You'd really like
to know whether or not he's single, wouldn't you?" The
words were hardly a question.

"Of course I would. It's not every day a girl finds a
man like that in her backyard. I wouldn't be human if I
hadn't noticed..." She cut her justification off with a
muttered, "This is ridiculous," and rose from the table
to retrieve the roll of masking tape from the counter.
"I'm a twenty-seven-year-old woman who's got better
things to do than think about some hunk who gets off on
buried bones, hates my dog and, for all I know, might
happen to be somebody's husband. He's probably not
even what I remember. I was awfully tired this morning."

Linda's brown eyes settled knowingly on Stephanie's
back. "That's the lamest excuse I've ever heard you come
up with."

"That's because I don't usually try to come up with
excuses. Maybe I'll get better with practice. Want to help
me paint?"

"Maybe later. I'm already late picking up the boys.
What I'd like to know is why you're getting so upset over
someone you don't seem to know a thing about. It's not
like you to fall for just a pretty face."

The agitation that had hit Stephanie so suddenly less-
ened with her deeply drawn breath. With a sigh, she knelt
down on the floor to finish taping the baseboard.
"Maybe it's just because it's been so long since a man

looked at me as if I was a woman. A reaction of the feminine ego?''

"I'll buy that last part, but you've got the other wrong. I've seen how men look at you and, believe me, it doesn't do a thing for my sagging ego."

Linda had recently turned thirty and was convinced she was entering her dotage. That's why her hair was now eight shades lighter than it had been two weeks ago.

"Remember when we were registering for that mythology class you conned me into taking with you?" she went on, only to interrupt herself. "That reminds me. That class starts next week, doesn't it? I'll need to get a sitter for the kids." Without missing a beat, she plunged ahead. "Anyway, I'd wager that half the males in the place were watching you at one time or another. It hasn't been a long time since a man's noticed you. It's just been a long time since you've noticed a man noticing you."

The ringing of the telephone saved Stephanie from having to acknowledge that piece of undeniably accurate insight. It had been over a year since she'd called off her engagement to Steve Elliot. Had it also been that long since she'd really paid any attention to men other than just as acquaintances? There were several single men in her circle of friends—a few of whom she'd dated off and on—but they were all just that. Friends.

"I'll be back later," Linda said, her glance flying to her watch as the phone rang again. Giving Zeus a quick pat and taking her cola with her, she hurried to the door. Her equally rushed "bye" followed her out.

Stephanie grabbed the phone. Her soft, somewhat absent hello was followed by the sound of a deep, very male voice.

"Ms. Moore? This is Adam Colter. I hope I'm not interrupting you."

The only thing being interrupted at the moment was her heartbeat, which for some reason had just skipped erratically. "No. I was just..." Just what? Her mind frantically questioned. Trying to figure out why I've been thinking about you? "No," she repeated decisively. "You're not interrupting."

"Good." That was the end of the preliminaries. "I said I'd get back to you with a schedule sometime tomorrow. Since I had to stop by my office, I thought I'd do it now. Summer-term classes start in a few days...on the...ah..." The rustle of paper came over the line. The pages of a calendar being turned?

"The seventeenth," she supplied, matching his businesslike tone.

The pause on the other end of the line seemed to change quality a little. "How'd you know that?"

"I'm taking a class myself."

"Whose?"

The man was definitely blunt. "Professor Mitchell's. Markham Mitchell."

"Never heard of him. What's his field?"

"Greek mythology," she answered, chalking up his interest to nothing more than curiosity about an unknown colleague. As she understood it, Professor Mitchell was on loan to UCLA from a university back East. She was about to mention that when the voice in her ear cut her off.

"Why are you taking that? It's not an education course. Didn't you say you're a counselor?"

The matter of her occupation had come up when he'd indicated that the inconvenience to her should be minimized because the excavation would be done while she was at work. She'd just as politely informed him that she didn't work during the summer. "Yes," she confirmed, "that's what I said. And I'm taking the course because I decided not to go to Greece."

"Because you decided not to go to Greece." The way he repeated her words made it sound like he was translating them from some obscure foreign language. "I'm sure there's a point to that, but I'm afraid I missed it."

The genuine puzzlement in his husky voice prompted her to elaborate. "I was going to go to Greece this summer, but I used my savings on my pool. The whole point of the trip was to see the places where the myths originated, and since I'm not doing that, I'm taking a course instead."

"Why?" he repeated.

The answer to that seemed perfectly clear to her. "Because I'm interested in it."

"I assumed that much. I was asking why you put in a . . . ah, sorry," he abruptly concluded. "We're getting a little off track here. I didn't mean to get personal."

She was pretty sure he'd wanted to know why she'd canceled her trip in favor of a pool. She was also grateful that he hadn't asked. Her decision to start being more practical had been a product of the same impulsive nature prompting the change, and she didn't think he'd understand her rather lopsided rationale. He struck her as the logical type.

"It's okay," she assured, acknowledging his last remark with good social grace.

"Is it?"

She stopped winding the phone cord around her finger. "Is it, what?"

"Okay to get personal."

Rarely did Stephanie have any difficulty holding up her end of a conversation. Even when she knew nothing about a subject, she could at least ask intelligent questions. Being totally unprepared for this particular conversational shift, however, she couldn't think of a thing to say.

Adam saved her the embarrassment of letting the three-second lapse increase into a long and awkward silence. He also quite effectively crushed the surge of anticipation she adamantly told herself she didn't feel. "I want to apologize for what happened earlier. I wouldn't have yelled at your mutt, er, your dog if he'd left the fossil alone. It's vitally important that each fragment remain exactly as it is until the entire site can be documented."

He called that an apology?

"I accept your apology, such as it was, Dr. Colter. I'll also remind you that I promised to keep Zeus out of your way. You just take care of Dino."

"Dino?"

"The dinosaur."

In a tone that clearly questioned her intelligence, he flatly stated, "It's not a dinosaur."

"I thought you said you couldn't tell what it was yet."

"I can't. But it's not a dinosaur. They lived during the Mesozoic era and died out at the end of the Cretaceous period. We've never found anything around here that's over forty thousand years old."

"Of course," she muttered. Didn't everybody know that? "How thoughtless of me."

Adam had the foresight to ignore her sarcasm and immediately changed the subject. It was a little annoying to think he might be laughing at her, but she could swear there was a smile in his voice. "If eight o'clock the morning of the nineteenth will be all right with you, we'll start the actual excavation then. There's some site preparation to be done first. I'll bring you a schedule tomorrow of the days I'll have students with me. There'll be a few days when I'll probably be alone, but you won't even known I'm there."

Adam had seriously underestimated Stephanie's intuitive powers.

Though the noise from her blow dryer made it impossible to hear anything, she knew his bright red sports car pulled up in front of her house even before she saw Zeus leap from the chair by her closet and dart down the hall. No one ever made it to the door before Zeus did.

The doorbell rang just as she dropped her brush on the dresser and grabbed a slash of pale aqua cotton from her canopy bed. "Damn," she muttered, pulling the T-shirt-style shift over her head. "Why couldn't he be late?"

He'd said he'd be here at eight. A quick glance at the old-fashioned brass clock on her nightstand indicated it was eight-nineteen—which, because her clock was fast, meant it was really seven fifty-nine. She'd had the feeling he was going to be the punctual type.

She was prepared to forgive him that, though. Just as she was prepared to overlook their less-than-auspicious beginning and start her association with Adam Colter on a strictly civilized level. Being a firm believer in the philosophy of making the best of a difficult situation, she really had no choice. *When life hands you lemons, make lemonade,* proclaimed the poster she kept in her office at school.

Stephanie didn't much care for lemonade, but it was the thought that counted.

Her freshly dried hair fell loosely around her shoulders as she gave her head a quick shake and turned to the mirror over her antique dresser. Because of the tan she'd acquired, she hadn't used any blush, but her cheeks seemed to have even more color than she'd noticed before. No doubt a result of all the rushing around she'd been doing. Squinting at her reflection, she remembered the second coat of mascara she'd intended to apply. It was too late for that now. At least she was dressed.

Congratulating herself on that feat, she took a deep breath and calmly stepped into the hall. Long ago she'd learned how to pull herself together in a hurry, then present a commendably unruffled appearance to the rest of the world. Very few people realized that she spent most of her time running five minutes late. Even when she allowed herself plenty of time, as she thought she had this morning, she invariably found herself behind schedule.

Zeus had planted himself in front of the door. Picking him up with a soft admonition to "Behave," she pulled the door open and found herself staring at a chest that appeared even broader than she'd remembered. Almost as if her subconscious needed to confirm what she thought she'd seen yesterday, her eyes started downward to take in the rest of his nicely constructed anatomy.

The only confirmation she got, though, was a fleeting impression of muscled biceps straining against the knit bands of a short-sleeved kelly-green polo shirt and a heavy camera bag slung over his shoulder. Both the inadvertent perusal and the pleasant "Good morning" she'd planned were sacrificed to a muffled "Hi" as she squeezed her eyes closed and rubbed the sudden itch in her nose.

"Hi, yourself," he greeted, chuckling, and reached into the back pocket of his faded jeans. He held out a folded sheet of paper. "This is a copy of the schedule I'll be using. Just wanted to give it to you before I started in out back. If you don't mind, I'll let myself in the side gate."

Stephanie had yet to look up at him. The tickling in her nose was verging dangerously close to a sneeze, and she was so busy trying to stifle it that she hadn't paid attention to anything else. "You can come through... ahh...ahh..." Jerking her head to the side, she gave in to the involuntary, and very inelegant, spasm. Then, another.

"Cold?" he inquired blandly.

"Allergy," she replied, feeling the attack subside.

"There's a lot of pollen in the air. The smog probably doesn't help, either."

"Oh, it's not that." Stepping back to complete the offer she hadn't quite verbalized, she motioned him inside. Since he didn't have a contingent of students with him, he might as well come through the house—this time anyway. "I'm allergic to dogs."

The tiny animal who'd recently taken to sleeping on Stephanie's extra pillow—thus causing her morning stuffiness—wasn't moving from his perch in her arms. She could feel his little muscles stiffening though and his low, throaty growl indicated that he wasn't too pleased with the man who'd just invaded his territory by stepping into the living room.

Catching a glimpse of the frown being directed at Zeus as she closed the door, and thinking it was because of the menacing noises her puppy was making, she offered a quick, conciliatory assurance. "Don't worry. He won't bite. He only *thinks* he's a Doberman."

The scowl etching the attractive lines around Adam's narrowed eyes was redirected at Stephanie. "I wasn't worried. I was just wondering why you have a dog if you're allergic."

"Because I like him," she returned simply, and saw his eyebrow arch in question. "You can come through this way."

Ignoring his perplexity, she led him past the living room with its profusion of plants, the mauve, ice-blue and pink pillows scattered along her white sofa and the brass chest she used for a coffee table, then came to a stop next to the painting supplies stacked up in the breakfast nook. "When will the rest of your crew get here?" she inquired, scratching Zeus behind his ear.

Adam's glance darted from the puppy glaring at him to the roller and brushes on the newspapers by the paint tray. From there, his inspection took in the plastic wadded up in the corner by a potted fig tree and the brass-framed poster she'd taken off the wall and laid on the table.

This part of the house was a mess. She'd managed to get all the walls and cabinets in the kitchen taped off yesterday afternoon, but only the baseboard along the counter had been painted. The chore was more tedious and time-consuming than she'd expected.

Apparently realizing that she was still waiting for an answer, but not yet finished with his survey, he absently said, "It'll just be me today, but I'll be bringing a few people with me tomorrow. The schedule I gave you sets it all out."

The low growl coming from her arms sounded a bit more threatening than Stephanie liked. Zeus had never reacted this way toward anyone. But, then, everyone adored him. Everyone except the man now staring at the tennis ball lying on the beige tiled floor. Zeus regarded tennis balls as his sole and exclusive property.

Rather than risk a confrontation that could only be catastrophic between beings she'd christened Zeus and

Apollo, Stephanie put the dog in the laundry room with his ball and a sincere "Sorry, fella." Thinking she'd make up for the indignity Zeus was being forced to suffer by barbecuing him a hamburger later, she stepped back into the kitchen and unfolded the paper she'd been given. Might as well take a look at this schedule of his.

Neat columns of squares covered most of the page. Inside each were the days, dates and times the people listed in each of them would make their appearance in her backyard. Several of the little squares had only the word "lecture."

A total of four weeks had been accounted for.

Thinking that some things were better handled when taken only one day at a time, she added the sheet to the stack of coupons and mail on the drainboard. "It looks like you have everything quite organized," she noted, figuring that Dr. Colter was probably the epitome of organization. Punctual people usually were, she concluded, seeing him glance at his watch. "What's on your agenda for this morning? The square for today just had "8:00 A.M." and a "p" written in it."

"That's my abbreviation for photos." His eyes flicked from his wrist to her stove, then back. "I believe your clock's fast."

"It is. By twenty minutes. I keep them all that way."

"Why?"

"So I won't be late." Smiling at his confusion, she added, "Later than I normally am, anyway."

Apparently her explanation lacked the logic he needed. "If you know you've got the extra time, what's the point?"

"I suppose it's psychological. What did you say you were going to do this morning?" Never discuss politics with a politician, she decreed to herself, or the inexplicable with a scientist.

There was a fair amount of amusement underlying Adam's rather puzzled expression. Rubbing his fingers along his jaw while he watched her take the empty glass pot from her coffee maker, he leaned against the counter. "All I'm going to do this morning is take some pictures and set a few stakes so the grid can be laid out. Does it really help to set your clocks ahead like that? I mean, don't you find yourself subtracting the extra minutes anyway?"

Keeping her back to him, she scooped the grounds into the filter. She hadn't had her coffee yet, and its preparation provided a good excuse to do something other than stand there wondering why that odd sensation in her stomach was back again. She'd been doing just fine until she'd seen the smile slip into his eyes.

"Sometimes I do," she responded to his question. Remembering the rule she'd just invented, she switched topics. "What's this grid you're talking about?"

"Nothing very complicated really. We mark two-meter units out with wooden stakes. Each stake is numbered by position and compass direction, then the units are excavated individually. Sometimes we have to break down a unit into four one-meter squares when we're finding a lot of fragments. The purpose in doing that is to accurately document the entire site."

She sighed. "No wonder this is going to take so long."

After that explanation she'd expected him to start out the back door. It sounded like he had a lot of work to do, and as he was the organized type, she doubted he'd want to waste his time in her kitchen. He wasn't moving from his position by the counter, though, and his camera bag was now resting on the beige surface. A quick glance over her shoulder found him staring at the brew just beginning to drip into the pot.

It would be terribly rude not to offer. "Would you like a cup?"

That darn dimple was back, only she wasn't the recipient of his decidedly charming smile. At least not for a few seconds. He was still staring at the machine beside her. "I was afraid you wouldn't ask. If you don't mind, I'd really appreciate one. I got in late last night and didn't have time to fix any this morning."

He was using the singular.

It was senseless to pretend that her curiosity about Adam wasn't killing her. After all, she was only human. But rather than resorting to one of those "subtly obvious" inquires, such as "Oh, didn't your wife have time, either?" she just set another mug next to the one she'd taken from the cabinet. Stephanie never had been able to pull off the blinking innocent look that kind of probing would require. "It won't take long."

"It's worth the wait. All I ever make at home is instant."

There was that singular again.

"Cream or sugar?"

"Since it's the real thing, I'll take it black."

Oh, to hell with it, she thought to herself, and was preparing to ask the terribly transparent question when she heard him moving back around the counter. Leaning across it to see what he was doing, she found him crouched on the other side inspecting the trim she'd started painting yesterday afternoon.

"I suppose one of the disadvantages of being a single female," he said, "is not having a man around to do repairs. For a bachelor, it's not having someone around who can make a decent pot of coffee. Is this a base coat?''

The way he was frowning at the pale peach paint at the bottom of the wall made her forget that the question she'd been about to ask had just been answered.

She frowned back at him. ''What do you mean?''

''Are you going to use a real color over this?''

''What's wrong with peach?''

''Well, nothing really. This just looked a little washed out and I thought...'' Looking a bit embarrassed, he drew himself up and offered what sounded like a definite attempt at compromise. ''You do nice work.''

If he'd looked a little less thoughtful as he glanced at the baseboard, she would probably have been quite offended with his criticism of her taste. As it was, it appeared very much like he was trying to comprehend the reason a person would prefer a pale pastel over a ''real'' color. She loved pastels and thought this particular shade perfectly lovely.

''The coffee's ready,'' she announced, diplomatically returning the conversation to the former subject. She held a lavender mug out to him. It had a rather ornate Pegasus on one side. She took the rose-colored one with the unicorn on it. It was her favorite because it almost matched the poster of the unicorn that usually hung on the wall. But for the moment that poster was lying facedown on the table.

As his large hand lifted to accept the pastel mug, she smiled to herself. ''Try to ignore the color.''

''You'll find there's very little I ignore,'' he stated quietly, then grinned in his coffee. ''But I'll try to make an exception in this case.''

''That's very flexible of you.''

"Yes," he returned, not quite able to look as serious as he sounded. "It is, isn't it?"

If she didn't know better, she could have sworn he was teasing her. But, then, she wasn't sure she did know better. Not really knowing the man, how could she possibly know when he was being serious and when he wasn't?

That thought was abandoned when he stepped back and slung the strap of his camera bag over his shoulder. Holding up his mug, he nodded toward the back door. "I'll just take this outside with me. You've obviously got things you want to do, and I don't want to hold you up any longer. It'll only take me an hour or so today, but I'll be back at eight tomorrow. Okay?"

Nodding, she took a sip of her coffee. He was going to be here for an hour? A whole hour.

"Oh, one other thing." Halting halfway across the kitchen, he turned and glanced around to find her staring at the front of his jeans.

Her ebony eyes widened as she sucked in a guilty breath and immediately clamped her bottom lip between her teeth. She'd been admiring how nicely the snug denim fitted his lean little posterior, and he'd turned around so quickly that she'd wound up staring at his zipper.

It was apparent that he was quite accustomed to having women treat themselves to an eyeful. It also seemed that, while he took the admiration in stride, he was quite adept at handling such a situation.

Somehow managing to appear as if he hadn't noticed where she'd been looking—even though she was painfully aware that he had—he gave her a laconic little smile. "Would you mind if I have my calls transferred to your phone while I'm working here?"

Determined to sound as nonchalant as she possibly could, she tilted her chin at a slightly arrogant angle. "I don't think that would pose a problem, Dr. Colter."

At the sound of the formality, his thick eyebrows quirked. "Stephanie," he said flatly. "You and I will be seeing each other just about every day for the next month. Undoubtedly during that time, I'll catch you some morning taking the garbage out in your bathrobe, and there may even be occasions when I'm running around in nothing more than cutoffs. Neither are exactly formal situations. I also imagine that at some point we may even carry on a conversation about something other than coffee, your unorthodox time-keeping, how the excavation of Dino is going or wall colors. Under those circumstances, don't you think you should call me Adam?"

Three

By the middle of the following week Adam wouldn't have blamed Stephanie if she'd called him every name in the book. Not only had he relegated her pip-squeak of a dog to the confines of the house—something that had to make her painting project much more difficult with the inquisitive animal underfoot—but her entire backyard now bore a definite resemblance to an archaeological dig, complete with grid work, sifting frames and an excavation crew of students. If something like that had happened to him, he'd never have been able to remain so calm. He liked his life ordered and organized. Something like this, he thought while instructing two of his students to keep their tools out of her flower beds, would have driven him nuts.

Adam wasn't exactly a member of the tea-and-textbook set many of his colleagues had pigeonholed themselves into, but he was far from the free-spirited soul he thought Stephanie to be. He likened her to an elusive butterfly. Not the colorful Monarch, but the delicate Spring Azure. All soft color darting from one place to the next without any seeming sense of direction. Yet, there was a contrasting element in her personality that gave her a very definite sense of purpose. He'd seen it while she'd been talking with some of his students yesterday after she'd come home from her class, again this morning when she'd brought bags of popcorn out to the half-dozen little neighborhood boys sitting on the fence to watch the excavation. Stephanie cared about people and, unlike most, she was willing to listen rather than talk. Few had that ability.

There were also few people who had the ability to so thoroughly confuse him. She was the singularly most disorganized person he'd ever met. Her thinking processes were completely baffling, and some of the things she did lacked any basis in rationality.

She also had the greatest pair of legs he'd ever seen.

It was those legs he was watching now. He could see her through the sliding glass doors of her dining room and her position wasn't doing a thing for his concentration. She was leaning across the counter with only her shorts-clad bottom and those incredible legs visible as she reached for something he couldn't see.

She was reaching for the phone. It was the third time in the past hour and a half that the thing had rung and, as she suspected, the call wasn't for her.

Placing the receiver on the counter, she mentally closed her eyes to the sight that greeted her when she reached the back door. Her yard was an absolute mess.

Naturally, the thing that had decided to bury itself out there—probably a dire wolf or saber-toothed cat, according to Adam—hadn't picked a spot near the center of the original hole. The result of that oversight was that the neat, kidney shape of her pool was now being systematically destroyed by Adam and a dozen or so T-shirt-and-jean-clad students.

Stephanie could cope with the kids and the inconvenience. What she was finding a bit annoying were all of Adam's phone calls. Every person who called him, male or female, seemed to know the exact moment she reached the top of her ladder.

The husky-voiced woman calling for Adam now wasn't the same one who'd called a few minutes ago. She definitely wasn't the breathy one who'd called yesterday, either. All three women, though, had seemed equally hesitant when they'd heard Stephanie answer. Not surprising since Adam had said the phone he'd put on call forwarding was the one in his apartment.

Halting Zeus's bid for freedom by scooping him up as he started past her legs, she smiled at the bespectacled young man making notes at her patio table. "Excuse me. Would you please tell Dr. Colter he has a call?"

With his index finger on the bridge of his glasses, the youth glanced up. Giving her a shrug, he cupped his hands around his mouth. "Dr. Colter! Telephone!"

"Thanks," she mumbled. She could have done that herself.

Rubbing the itch in her nose, she nudged the door closed with her foot and gave Zeus an affectionate squeeze. "Come on punkin'. The playboy professor's on his way in, so it's into the playpen with you."

There was no way Stephanie was going to lock Zeus in the laundry room every time Adam came in to use the phone. The only alternative she'd been able to come up with had been to borrow a playpen Linda had stashed in her attic. It was now in Stephanie's living room next to the ladder.

There was an added benefit to that particular solution. With Zeus safely occupied inside the pen with his dog biscuits and tennis ball, Stephanie didn't have to worry about him eating her paintbrushes.

The back door opened and closed, and a moment later she heard Adam answer his call with a slightly distracted, "Dr. Colter."

Back up on the ladder, Stephanie dipped her roller in the paint tray, wondering if the action she was contemplating would be terribly rude. When the phone had rung, she'd lowered the volume of the stereo. Now, she wanted to turn it up so she didn't have to eavesdrop on the conversation taking place around the corner. Humming along with the song she could barely hear didn't help. Though she was trying not to listen—sort of—she could quite clearly discern every word Adam was saying.

"I can't tonight, Diane. How about Wednesday after I finish up at school? Let's make it doubles. If you can get a court, I'll pick you up at three."

He'd just switched the woman's request for a singles match to doubles and from evening to midafternoon. In a way, that seemed to confirm Stephanie's suspicions. Given the fact that he had so many girlfriends, it was obvious enough that no particular one of them held his exclusive interest.

Though she'd tried to forget her initial comparison, she couldn't help thinking that Adam bore more than just a physical resemblance to the mythical Apollo. Just like the god, he had more than his share of lovers. Was the breathy Cindy the equivalent of the nymph Dryope? Was the efficient-sounding Barbara his Cyrene? No, she decided. The woman he was talking to about tennis, Diane, more closely compared with that fabled huntress, since she was probably the athletic type.

What would it take to capture his full attention, she wondered, hearing his absent, "Great, see you then." Of course, she wasn't thinking of herself in terms of trying to do that. Joining a chorus line wasn't her idea of a sharing relationship—and the fact that her knees turned to putty every time he looked at her had nothing to do with anything. She was trying to ignore that anyway.

"Damn," she muttered, jerking her thoughts back to her task. While she'd been allowing her mind to wander, her roller had wandered too close to the ceiling.

The expletive was silently repeated when she reached for the old towel that was no longer next to the paint tray. It was on the plastic at the base of the ladder. So was Adam.

"I'll get it."

"That's okay. I'll . . ."

Stephanie had already reached the bottom rung. Caught mid-descent, she'd turned halfway around just as Adam bent over. His shoulder, connecting with her hip, knocked them both sideways.

Jerking back up to steady her when she instinctively grabbed for him, Adam chuckled. "Easy there. I said I'd get it for you. You've probably made enough trips up and down this thing already."

Since she'd regained her footing on the bottom rung, there was absolutely no reason why she shouldn't let go of his shoulders. She was in no danger of falling, yet she still felt slightly off balance. Even her voice sounded a little shaky when she mumbled, "One or two."

It didn't take much to figure out that her precarious feeling had something to do with the way his hands had splayed around her waist—and the fact that he hadn't released her, though his grip had eased considerably.

From her vantage point of approximately one foot away, she saw his clear blue eyes settle on her mouth. Then, with the slow blink of his lashes, the same, puzzled amusement she'd seen before crept across his chiseled features.

"You okay?" he asked, stepping back to watch her bare feet hit the floor.

The oddly electric sensation she'd felt when he touched her seemed to have short-circuited her vocal cords. Her only response was a slight nod as she locked her knees.

Adam didn't seem to notice either her lack of verbal finesse or the puppy growling behind him. Rubbing his chin, he took another step back. His eyes traveled quickly up the length of her legs, skipped over the baggy old shirt she'd salvaged from her mom's Goodwill box, then settled easily on hers.

"I'm sorry about all these phone calls, Stephanie. If it wasn't so important that I be available to Dave and everyone else involved while we're working on the text for the Arizona dig, I wouldn't have my calls transferred here. It'll be ready to go to the publisher in a couple of weeks, and as soon as it is, I'll stop having my calls transferred."

The majority of his calls *had* been from a Dr. Dave Abrahms and, apparently having been told by Adam what the circumstances were around there, he had apologized profusely for the interruptions. She therefore overlooked those mollifying circumstances in favor of a little good-natured teasing. "You don't have to do that on my account. Heaven forbid that I should have the demise of your social life on my conscience. Just out of curiosity," she continued, picking up the rag to wipe the paint from her fingers, "do you have a schedule with little boxes on it for all your girlfriends, too?"

Oh, Lord, she groaned to herself. Did that sound as bitchy as she thought?

Adam's brow pinched. "Of course I don't. And the women I know are just . . . friends."

"You don't have to explain anything to me," she returned breezily. "I'm just the answering service."

"I'm not trying to explain anything," he muttered, knowing quite well he was doing just that. What he didn't understand was why.

Uncomfortable with that inexplicable phenomenon, he opted for a change of subject. It was something he'd meant to mention anyway. "When it's just me working out back, would you mind turning your stereo either up or down?"

"I beg your pardon?"

"Either turn it up so I can hear it better or turn it down so I can't hear it at all. The way you usually have it, all I'm getting is the bass and it's driving me crazy trying to figure out which song is playing."

"What would you prefer?"

"I'd like up, but not enough so you give the whole neighborhood a Johnny Mathis concert. I happen to like his stuff, though, so if you wouldn't mind . . ." Allowing his slightly crooked smile to complete his request, he held out his hand. "Give me your rag. You've got paint on your nose."

She didn't give it to him. He took it—and she found herself staring straight ahead at his chest. He'd stepped right in front of her, and his hand had just pushed under her hair to cup the back of her neck. "Hold your head up," he instructed, sliding his thumb along her jaw to tip her chin. "From what I've heard so far, your collection's better than mine. Do you have all his albums?"

"Whose?" she swallowed.

"The man whose music we're discussing."

"Oh, him." She was only vaguely aware of the low, melodic tones coming from the speakers behind her. Though the song was barely audible, she immediately recognized the lead-in to *Chances Are*. Was there a message in that?

Hardly. Chances were that what Adam was doing meant absolutely nothing. He was just being...what? she asked herself, watching him concentrate on the paint splatter on her face.

All of his attention seemed centered on his self-appointed chore. The seriousness of his expression gave no indication at all that he found anything unusual about his actions.

He's being unfair, she finally determined. And the odd part about that was that he didn't even know it. As impossible as it was, he didn't seem to know how truly devastating his touch could be. Being this close to him, feeling the gentle strength of his hands, inhaling the clean scent of the wood soap he used was making her acutely aware of the powerful aura of sensuality surrounding this man. Was this a test? Had some god become bored in his heavens and decided to see just how much she could take?

You're being ridiculous, she scolded herself, staring up at the man looming over her.

The growing intensity in his expression removed the last trace of innocence from his actions. There was something primitive about the way his eyes seemed to darken as they quietly roamed her still features. His hand had stopped its motion, and she barely noticed that the rag had fallen to the floor. She was conscious only of the slight motion of his thumb on her cheek, the feel of his fingers pressing the back of her neck and the way his gaze had settled on her mouth.

Adam was conscious of a different set of sensations. The slight part of her lips seemed to invite the pressure of his own. Her skin, smooth beneath his thumb, felt even softer than he'd imagined. It had been a mistake to touch her.

You, he said silently to her as his gaze lowered to the gentle curve of her breasts, are one very dangerous lady, Stephanie Moore.

She probably thought the faded old cotton shirt she was wearing over her shorts provided adequate coverage. And it had, until he'd touched her. Now, by the way her nipples pushed against the soft fabric he could tell she wasn't wearing a bra. The fact that he might have caused that kind of physical reaction told him far more than did the dark eyes cautiously meeting his.

Knowing that if he stood there for another second he'd wind up kissing that beautiful mouth, he cleared his throat and stepped back. "Have you had lunch?"

Her hand moved toward her cheek, but she abruptly halted the motion and curled her fingers at her side. "Uh . . . no, I haven't. Why?"

"Because I haven't, either. It's almost two, and I'm hungry. The kids'll be clearing out in a while, so why don't I go pick us up some hamburgers. What do you want on yours?"

He wasn't giving her a chance to refuse. Stephanie wasn't paying any attention to that, though. She was too busy trying to salvage what was left of her composure and act as nonchalant as he was. There was no doubt in her mind that Adam had been about to kiss her. Telling herself that she hadn't wanted him to was a lie she couldn't quite manage. "I'll take one with everything and one plain."

"You want two?"

"One's for Zeus."

At the sound of his name, the puppy's little ears perked up. The mention of hamburgers had already stopped his ineffective growls and started his tail wagging.

Adam eyed the playpen. "Does he want fries?"

"No. But I do. A large order." Maybe by the time he got back the knot in her stomach would have disappeared and there'd be room for the food.

Zeus got fries after all. Stephanie was almost positive that the extra order Adam returned with after the students had departed was a peace offering. On the other hand, Adam's motives could have been more selfish. With the pup sleeping off his lunch, Adam could eat his without being growled at. Stephanie noted that among Adam's other "faults," he was also quite practical.

With Stephanie's back to him while she cleared the table, Adam allowed his eyes to roam up and down the length of her bare legs while he talked about the progress being made unearthing Dino. It was because of his preoccupation that he failed to notice Stephanie's lack of coloring.

She'd gotten awfully quiet when he mentioned the part about not having found one foreleg and lowered herself to one of the chairs when he said that the skull was still missing. It was about that time that his eyes finally settled on her face, and he noticed how pale she'd become. Rather than risk the obvious consequences of continued discussion on that subject, he prepared to switch to one he considered more superfluous. There was no point mentioning that what had been uncovered so far didn't quite resemble anything he'd ever seen before.

Flipping through the pages of the textbook she'd left sitting on the peach-and-cream place mat next to him, Adam's brow furrowed. "Why are you so interested in mythology?"

Appreciating his obvious attempt to take her mind off the unappetizing images floating through it, she smiled weakly. "Because it fascinates me."

"What's so fascinating about it?"

Even if the knot in her stomach had gone away, which it hadn't, she couldn't have eaten now. Not after all this talk about bones and skulls. She pushed her hamburger toward him. His was already gone. "I suppose it's because an entire civilization based itself on those myths and legends, and that civilization is the basis for our own...along with things like medicine, mathematics, philosophy and language."

"A statement like that needs examples."

"Isn't it enough to just state my thesis without proving it?"

"Nope."

She didn't think it would be. Someone like Adam would always want proof. This was one instance where she could give it to him. "The most obvious example is something we use everyday. A good portion of our own language can be attributed to the gods. Pan's shouts for joy caused the Titans to flee. That's where 'panic' comes from. Chronos, the father of the gods, gave his name to time...chronology...and things that occur over a period of time are described as chronic."

The thoughtful frown on his face after he'd swallowed another french fry seemed to indicate that he was listening. His eyes weren't on hers, though. He was looking at her mouth. "So it's really the influence of myths and not the myths themselves you're interested in. That makes more sense.''

"I don't know what you mean by making more sense, but it *is* the mythology I'm interested in. Specifically, the lineage. You know, who's related to whom and the circumstances of each god or goddess's birth.''

Any comprehension he may have managed vanished. With a slow blink he pulled his eyes from the full curve of her lips and leaned back in his chair. "You don't really believe that stuff, do you?''

"That depends on which part of it you're talking about. Yes, I think it all existed in people's minds. No, I don't believe that a being named Aphrodite sprang from sea foam created by a primal murder.''

He looked relieved. "So you admit it's illogical?''

Stephanie frowned. "Why does it have to be logical?''

"How can you understand something that's not?''

"Not what?''

Exasperation tinged his tone. "Not logical, Stephanie. If you're going to base your arguments on the Greek civilization, then you've got to consider all of it. The Greek intellect was undisciplined and chaotic until Aristotle . . . a Greek mind you . . . created the science of logic.''

"Why are you getting so upset?''

"I'm not upset.''

"Well, you sound like it to me. Do you get this way during your classes, too?''

He grinned. "Sometimes.''

"I thought so.''

"And I think you're a reasonably intelligent woman, so you've got to realize that none of that mythology stuff makes any sense.''

There was obviously no way she could explain her contrasting point of view to his satisfaction, so there was no point in trying. Remember your rule, she reminded herself, trying very hard not to smile at his confusion. She had the feeling he didn't like being confused.

It occurred to her just then, that she enjoyed making him that way.

"To someone like you, I don't suppose it does," she conceded graciously.

"What's 'someone like me' supposed to mean?"

"You're a scientist."

"You make my profession sound like something I should apologize for."

There was something about his smile that she hadn't really noticed before; the hint of self-mockery in it indicating that he didn't take himself too seriously. She liked that.

"Did anyone ever tell you you're a very puzzling lady?"

"I can't say anyone ever has," she returned, feeling the lump in her stomach slide to her throat. The way his eyes kept shifting from her eyes to her mouth was terribly disconcerting.

"There's something that's always fascinated me."

"What's that?"

"Puzzles."

The ring of the telephone provided her with a perfect excuse to avoid the slightly wicked gleam in his eyes. She'd tried to ignore the odd tension running just beneath the surface of their easy conversation, but it was much easier to do when there was some distance between them. A few dozen feet seemed appropriate. She picked up the wrappings from their lunch. "You might as well answer it since you're in here. It's for you anyway."

Barely catching the slight lift of his eyebrows, she disposed of the trash and strolled into the living room.

"Hello," she heard him say as she skirted the plastic-draped sofa. "Huh? Oh, yes it is. Just a second and I'll get her."

She raised her eyes to the ceiling. Naturally, she'd had him answer the only call she'd received all day.

Reentering the kitchen, she found him leaning against the counter, his long legs crossed at the ankle. Rather than handing the phone to her, he switched the receiver to his other ear. "No, you're not," he was saying. "You're not interrupting anything. We just finished lunch."

"Who is it?" she mouthed, wondering at how comfortably he was talking to someone he couldn't possibly know.

Holding up his index finger, his brow pinched while he listened to whoever it was on the other end of the line.

"No problem. She's right here." Holding out the receiver, he gave a hitchhiker motion with his thumb toward the window over the sink. "It's your neighbor. The one with the kids who're always hanging over the fence."

Adam was already walking out the back door by the time Stephanie had taken the phone and heard Linda's rather droll inquiry. "Before I get to the favor I want to ask, you want to tell me why Adonis is answering your phone?"

"It's Apollo, er, Adam," Stephanie corrected, scowling at the back door. "And he answered the phone because I thought it was for him. What's the favor?"

"He's really got incredible shoulders."

"What?"

"Adam. He just took his shirt off."

"How do you know that?"

"I can see him from the window. I'm upstairs in the den. Oh, my. His chest is even better than his back."

"Linda," Stephanie teased, fighting the urge to saunter over to her own window. "May I remind you that you're a married woman."

"Married, yes. Dead, no. Oh, damn. He just disappeared. Well, back to the reason I called. Do you think you could pick the boys up from softball practice tomorrow and keep them at your house for an hour or so? Ed's got some clients coming in from Florida, and since he'll be tied up, I've got to get 'em from the airport. I made them promise they'd behave . . . the kids, not the clients."

The next morning Stephanie was wishing there was some way to extract a similiar promise from her car when she tried to start it. Watching Linda's boys wouldn't be a problem, but she had to go get them first—which she couldn't do until the car decided to cooperate.

Refusing to panic, she slid from the little M.G. and stared at the unopened hood. A moment later, right on schedule, Adam's car pulled up at the curb. "Problems?" he asked, coming up behind her.

"This thing's always breaking down," she muttered, feeling the rest of what she was going to say stick in her throat when she turned around.

The bright Hawaiian print shirt he was wearing wasn't buttoned, and the way his hands were planted on his hips held the sides back to expose a broad expanse of tanned chest. A light arc of golden hair flaired between his flat male nipples, tapering down to disappear below the low waistband of his cutoffs.

"Oh, hell," she sighed, averting her glance to her watch. He wasn't playing fair. "I'm supposed to pick Linda's boys up in five minutes."

A teasing light crept into his eyes. "You sure it isn't twenty-five minutes? Or fifteen minutes ago?"

From the dull look she leveled at him, it was apparent she was in no mood to be teased. Shrugging, he pushed his hand into the pocket of his snug cutoffs and tipped his head toward his car. "Can you drive a stick?"

"I learned to drive on Dad's pickup, but it's been a while. Why?"

"Here." Extracting his keys, he picked up her hand and folded her fingers around them. "Take mine."

She didn't have time to refuse, or to tell herself that she hadn't felt the heat from Adam's hand all the way to the tips of her toes. Adam, shaking his head, was already walking toward the gate—and if she didn't leave right now, she'd never make it. The last thing she wanted to do was have those poor kids think they'd been stranded at the park when no one arrived to meet them.

Within an hour of her return, however, all hell broke loose, and Stephanie felt that leaving them stranded might not have been such a bad idea. She'd told the boys that they could watch what was going on out back but only if they stayed out of Adam's way.

According to Adam's schedule for today, he was only working with a couple of volunteers. Those two young men, both wearing the studious, introspective look that had probably earned each of them the label "nerd," had ignored the two boys Adam had finally allowed into the inner sanctum of the hole. So far, the five "men" had been tolerating each other in relative peace.

To Stephanie's surprise, Adam had shown an amazing amount of patience by answering the thousand and one questions Matthew, Linda's nine-year-old, kept asking him. Adam had even assigned Matthew and his seven-year-old brother, Micky, their own pile of dirt—one that had already been sifted through the large screen set up at the shallow end of the hole—so they could "help." It was apparent from what she could hear happening out there now that Adam was regretting his generosity.

"Hey! You kids get back from there," she heard him shout. "You've got your own pile."

"But Matthew won't let me dig in it," Mickey whined.

"There's enough dirt there for both of you. Matthew! Move over."

"Take it easy," she yelled out the back door, blocking Zeus's exit with her foot. "Matthew, you and Mickey just sit up on the fence and watch. I said you could go out there if you behaved, but if you're going to argue, you'll have to come in. Got it?"

Two curly brown heads lowered as the boys dropped the little shovels Adam had given them. Muttering to each other, they headed for the five-foot block wall separating the two backyards. She wasn't sure, but it sounded like Matthew had just called Mickey a crybaby.

Not waiting to see if her solution met with Adam's approval, she shut the door and opened a cabinet. What the boys probably needed was to be fed. It was already past lunchtime. Since Linda hadn't shown up yet, peanut butter and jelly sandwiches seemed to be in order.

Adam poked his head inside the back door. "Can't those kids stay in here?"

"What's the matter?" she inquired, lining slices of bread on the counter. "Don't you like children?"

"I love children. I adore children. I was a child once myself. But the kid with the braces is throwing dirt clods at—"

"I'm gonna tell Mom!"

"What's going on here?" came the familiar, strident voice of Eleanor Dobbs from somewhere along the side of the house.

Adam spun around just as Zeus shot out the door. "Herbert," he shouted at one of the students. "Stop that dog!"

"Oh, good grief," Stephanie sighed, jamming her hair behind her ears as she hurried after Adam. The boys were sitting on the fence threatening each other with the dire consequence of informing their mother of the other's transgressions. Nosy old Eleanor was standing on tiptoe at the back gate, trying to see into the hole. And the young man Adam had addressed as Herbert was trying his best not to trip as he chased Zeus through the maze of gridwork he'd been slogging away in. Zeus had just taken possession of one of the little shovels the boys had dropped.

"Do we have a problem here?" the gray-haired woman at the gate inquired.

"No, Mrs. Dobbs," Stephanie said quite calmly. "Everything's under control."

"Doesn't look like it to me. Why was that man yelling at Linda's boys?"

"Probably because they were in his way," Linda suddenly replied from behind her. Leaning against the gate, she frowned at her sons. "Matthew. Micky. Home. Now."

Watching Herbert feint to the left as Zeus lunged to the right, Stephanie saw Adam throw his hands in the air. She didn't hear what he said, though, and it was probably just as well. "The boys are just hungry, Linda. I was getting ready to give them lunch. Adam! Don't chase him!"

"Well, how in the hell else am I supposed to get that back?"

"It's only a shovel, for Pete's sake."

"It's not a shovel. It's a trowel."

Herbert was waving excitedly at his bespectacled partner. "He's taking it inside, Ronald!"

Raising her eyes to the heavens, Stephanie muttered, "See you later, Mrs. Dobbs," and heading toward the house, saw Adam disappear through the back door. Why were these guys getting so excited about a shovel anyway?

She'd told Adam before that it was pointless to chase Zeus, which was exactly what he was doing as he ran down the hall. Dog and pursuer turned a sharp right into her bedroom.

"He's trying to bury it under the bed." Not bothering to look up as Stephanie joined him on the floor, Adam peered under the ivory eyelet bedspread. "Good God. What all's he got under there?"

"Looks like a spool of thread, two balls, a Frisbee and my tennis shoe. I was wondering where that had disappeared to." Lying flat on her stomach, she inched forward to reach under the bed. Zeus dragged his newest prize farther away and started chewing on its handle. "Come on, punkin. Move back over here."

Adam was now lying on his stomach, too, only his attention wasn't on the puppy guarding his little stash. "Let him have it," he said quietly.

It wasn't what he'd said that made Stephanie abandon her attempts at retrieval, though Adam's abrupt dismissal of their pursuit was a bit unexpected. It was the feel of his hands when they settled around her waist, and the fact that he was pulling her out from under the bed.

A moment later, she looked over to see him propping himself up on his elbow. His eyes were running a slow, deliberate path from the curve of her hip, where his free hand still rested, to the pulse skipping at the base of her throat. She felt his fingers flex against the fabric of her shorts, then move up to settle on her side.

The breath she drew seemed to have caught somewhere short of its destination. The one he slowly exhaled when he pulled her closer fanned the wisps of hair on her cheek.

"I've got to do this, Stephanie."

Four

Adam's eyes locked on hers, intent gleaming in their cool blue depths. A moment ago, his fingers had trailed lightly over her rib cage. Now they curved around the back of her neck. There was no doubt as to what he was about to do, and no time to question the wisdom of letting him.

"Shh," he breathed against her lips, anticipating her protest. "Just let me kiss you."

She didn't move. She couldn't. The feel of his mouth brushing hers was a force so debilitating that nothing on earth could have pulled her away. If anything, that force was drawing her to him, allowing him to turn her into his chest to cradle her against him.

Never would she have imagined a kiss could be so tender, or so seductive. The warmth of his breath mingled with hers as her lips parted beneath his gentle urging. Slowly he traced the smooth membrane inside her upper lip with the tip of his tongue, then continued that sensuous foray along the edges of her teeth before entering the moist darkness of her mouth. Despite his deliberate lack of urgency, or maybe because of it, the little shocks darting inward from where his chest teased her breasts began to quicken. The ones racing from the slow circles his hand was pressing to her back had gone completely haywire.

She had no choice but to kiss him back, to join the exploration that was both tentative and erotically bold. It was as if some power beyond her had decreed that this man would waken her senses and make her feel the things she'd feared would never be hers.

There was something rather alarming about that realization.

She wasn't quite sure what that something was, and now wasn't the time for introspection. Zeus had just grown bored with his toy.

Adam's faint moan echoed the one that caught in her throat when she turned her head. He obviously regarded the pup's reappearance and the high-pitched yip announcing his presence as an intrusion. Stephanie was thinking of it more in terms of a rescue.

The lower half of Zeus's furry little body was still under the bed, a veil of beige eyelet lace draped over his head. Blinking up at Adam with what might have been a disapproving air, had a dog been capable of such an expression, he plopped his paw over Stephanie's hand.

Adam's voice was decidedly strained. "Is he the only male I'll have to fight off?"

"Fight off?" she repeated, wondering if she sounded as breathless as she felt.

Adam's hand settled on her cheek. His thumb moved slowly over her bottom lip. "Is there someone who might like to rearrange my face for doing what I just did?"

He didn't sound particularly worried. He did, however, look very much as if he was about to repeat what he'd just done.

Adam's lips were only a breath away when Zeus shot between their prone bodies. The back door had just opened, and a rather excited voice came from just inside the kitchen. "Dr. Colter? Can you come out here?"

With a barely audible oath, Adam muttered, "Your timing's incredible, Herbert," and dropped his hand. "I'll be there in a minute," he called back, swinging his long legs around to sit in front of her. His eyes narrowed. "Well?"

Watching Zeus curl up between her legs was just an excuse to keep her head lowered. She wasn't afraid to look at Adam. She just feared what he might see in her expression. "Well, what?"

Exasperated, Adam's jaw clenched, but his tone was quiet. "Is there someone?"

A slight shake of her head accompanied her soft no.

"I didn't think there was." Using the tips of his fingers, he tipped her face toward him. "At least not someone important to you."

"Why do you say that?"

"Because I don't think you would have responded to me like that if you were involved with another man."

The hint of arrogance in his statement, not to mention its accuracy, put her on the defensive. "With a man," she corrected calmly. "'Another' makes it sound like I'm involved with you, which . . ."

"You are," he completed for her.

"Which I'm not," she countered.

"That's what you think." Leaning forward, he captured her mouth in a kiss clearly designed to refute her denial.

If Stephanie'd had just a few more seconds, she would have been able to control the instantaneous explosion of desire he caused to course through her. Instead of leaning toward him, she could have twisted away and insisted, to herself anyway, that the feel of his mouth moving against hers and the heat radiating downward from where his hands rested on her shoulders wasn't the most exquisite thing she'd ever experienced. She didn't have those seconds, though.

"Dr. Colter!" the impatient student repeated, and Adam pulled back with a sigh.

Lifting himself to his feet, he held out his hand. "We'll continue this discussion later. Come on. I'll help you up."

When she ignored his offer of an assist, he simply shrugged and turned around.

Damn him! she silently swore as he disappeared into the hall. How dare he walk out of here grinning like that!

Adam usually knocked off work around three in the afternoon. It was now four-thirty, and it didn't look like he was in any hurry to wrap things up for the day. Whatever it was that Herbert had found was definitely keeping him busy.

Stephanie was trying to stay occupied herself. The physical part of that task was easy enough to manage. There were plenty of things needing to be done. It was the mental part that didn't have the luxury of choice.

Since it was apparent that Adam was going to occupy her thoughts, whether she wanted him to or not, she was trying to focus on any aspect of him other than the way he made her feel. The one she was concentrating on now helped considerably.

He'd sounded quite satisfied to find out that she wasn't involved with anyone. Yet *he* had women stacked up like a holding pattern over L.A. International. Talk about the old double standard.

"The list is getting longer," she muttered to Zeus who was trailing behind her as she carried an armload of clothes to the utility room. "That's just one more thing to prove how little we have in common."

Without quite realizing it, she had been making a mental catalog of their differences—out of a sense of self-preservation, she supposed. It was one thing to be attracted to someone, but another matter entirely to let that attraction develop into something that could never work in the first place.

She'd reluctantly allowed that maybe Adam was right about her already being involved with him. Not in the way he'd meant, but as Webster's defined the term: to occupy absorbingly; to cause to be concerned.

Well, her present train of thought proved the former, and the way she responded to him definitely fit the category of the latter. So what if the way he'd kissed her made her feel things she'd never really felt before? She and Adam were poles apart in their attitudes and thinking and, when it came right down to it, that was that kind of thing that could make or destroy a relationship. Wasn't it?

Dismissing the question tagging her conviction, she decided to tell him the only things he had a right to around here were the bones in her backyard. He could leave hers alone. She'd inform him of this, politely of course, just as soon as Herbert and Ronald left and Adam stopped playing in the dirt.

Stephanie ultimately didn't have a chance to tell Adam anything. She was coming up her front walk, having retrieved her afternoon paper from the low shrubs lining it, when the clink of the metal latch preceded Adam's exit through the side gate. Herbert and Ronald were right behind him.

"...puts the find in a different light," Adam was saying to his attentive students. "It's rare for this hemisphere, but explicable considering the..."

"Considering what, Dr. Colter?" the young man with the glasses prodded when Adam stopped both the explanation and his progress toward the cars parked at the curb.

Still keeping his eyes on Stephanie, Adam hurried on. "Considering the migration patterns during that period. I'll go into it more during class on Monday."

Realizing that they'd just been dismissed, Herbert and Ronald turned to the old sedan in front of Adam's Porsche, their heads bent over a yellow notepad.

"Finally finished for the day?" Directing the casual inquiry over her shoulder, Stephanie waved to Mrs. Dobbs, who was looking out her front window.

"Not quite." Adam waved at Mrs. Dobbs, too, and the nosy old lady immediately disappeared—no doubt to take up her position from some other vantage point. "Herbert found something that's made me a little curious about Dino. I think I'll work a while longer, if you don't mind."

The consternation in Adam's voice almost made Stephanie ask what it was that Herbert had found. The way his narrowed eyes were moving slowly between her knees and her neck as she turned around made her change her mind. The less time she spent with him, the better off she'd be.

"Suit yourself," she said with a shrug, and started past him. His hand closing around her upper arm allowed her only one step, though.

"But before I get to that," he continued as if she hadn't said anything, "I'd like to talk to you."

The feel of his hand, warm against her bare skin, was making an absolute mockery of the indifference she was striving to maintain. It was bad enough when he looked at her as though her T-shirt and shorts were transparent, but when he was this close...

The voice piercing the momentary silence was welcomed cause to abandon the analysis of Adam's effect on her nervous system.

"Hi!" Linda called brightly, jogging across the driveway, "all I want's some baking soda and then I'll... Oh, boy," she concluded, almost to herself when she saw Adam's hand slide down Stephanie's arm.

"Then you'll what?" Stephanie urged, wishing she didn't sound quite so grateful for the interruption.

"Ah... get out of your way."

It was apparent from the resignation tightening Adam's mouth that both the words and the intent were too late. "You're not in our way. I was just going back." Nodding to Linda, he quietly informed Stephanie that "We'll talk later."

Stephanie said nothing. She merely pulled her eyes from the determination in his and stared down at her paper as he walked away.

"Oh, Adam," Linda called after him, "thanks for all the time you spent with the boys today. You can't believe how they kept going on about getting to help you dig up your skeleton."

"No problem. They're good kids." They had been good—up to a point.

If the praise pleased their mother, Adam didn't notice. When he'd turned around, his glance had immediately settled on Stephanie and he'd yet to pull it away. The very elemental awareness he'd seen in her eyes when he'd touched her was still there, though somewhat masked by relief for her neighbor's presence.

"That's nice of you to say," he heard Linda answer, laughing, "considering how cranky they got on you. I'd like to apologize."

"No need. Stephanie explained they were just hungry, and I can certainly appreciate that. All males can get a little impatient when their appetites aren't satisfied."

The way Stephanie's dark eyes widened told Adam that his remark had found its target. Not at all certain how that remark came out of his mouth, he mumbled a quick "See you later," to Linda and hurried off to seek the sanctuary of the backyard. There was a puzzle at the bottom of the hole waiting to be solved. Yet, it was the puzzle of Stephanie Moore that he found more troublesome.

Had she been as shaken as he was by the impact of that one, simple kiss? he wondered to himself.

Walking down the broad plank sloping into the hole, he hunched down beside the fifteen inches of foreleg Herbert had uncovered and stared at the hoof that had also been exposed. The possibility of the fossil being that of a mammal once indigenous to the area no longer seemed probable.

Did she know how wonderful her body had felt against his?

The grayed bone he was looking at resembled the tibia of a horse, only a horse didn't have cloven hoofs. What he needed to do was find the skull. If he could only . . .

Running his fingers through his hair, he told himself that if he could only stop thinking about Stephanie, he might be able to get to work. Then he could come up with a logical explanation for what he was seeing. With a sigh of resignation, he sat down in the dirt. Coming up with a plausible reason for the effect Stephanie had on him was something else he should probably do.

There was something about her puzzling and amazingly quick mind that he'd found far more interesting than in Barbara's analytical intelligence. And her subtle sensuality, infinitely more compelling than Cindy's overt sexiness, had him completely intrigued—not to mention slightly frustrated. If for no other reason than to maintain his sanity, he had to discover why she'd so thoroughly invaded his thoughts. It didn't take much to figure out why he wanted to take her to bed.

As with any problem, the only way to discover the answer was to dissect the subject. Once each aspect of the issue was analyzed and understood, then the overall picture would fall into place. Quite simple, really. If it took making love with her to find his answer, well . . .

The scientific approach fell apart there. There was nothing at all clinical about the unnamed feelings he had for Stephanie, and Adam had the strangest premonition that any discovery he might make wouldn't be about her, but about himself.

Reaching for one of the small brushes used to flick bits of debris from the specimen, Adam quietly chuckled in dismissal. He didn't believe in premonitions.

Stephanie did, though, and the one filling her with a vague sense of unease when Adam had turned and walked away had danger written all over it. That was why she'd sent Linda into the house to help herself to the baking soda while she'd stayed out front. Adam probably wouldn't want to work for more than a couple of hours, and she could occupy herself for that long right here. Keeping a whole house between them had suddenly seemed like a very good idea.

"I don't believe this," Linda clucked as her thongs plopped down the steps. "You've got that beautiful man in your backyard, and you're out here in the front pulling weeds?" Clearly not comprehending how something like that could be possible, she shook her head. "Well, at least that proves something."

"Like I'm trying to avoid him?" Stephanie offered helpfully.

"That, too. But I was thinking more along the lines of it giving you something in common besides a mutual affection for old Johnny Mathis songs. You both have a strong affinity for dirt. Well," she continued, smiling at Stephanie's frown while she stepped over the small pile of weeds on the sidewalk, "best get myself back to the kitchen. You know, Stephanie, that man would be the perfect cure for a boring summer."

That thought had already occurred to Stephanie, and though she was inclined to agree with her friend's prescription, she knew she could never have just an affair. With Adam, that's all she could hope for. After all, they had so little to build anything on. Just look at how much she and her ex-fiancé, Steve, had had in common—and things still hadn't worked out for them. They'd agreed on practically everything.

But the magic had been missing. The magic she'd felt in Adam's arms. That strange, heady excitement had never found its place in her very comfortable, predictable relationship with Steve.

There has to be a compromise somewhere, she told herself, yanking at a particularly stubborn dandelion. Why was it that she'd found the magic in the man who so closely resembled a myth, when a nice, understandable mortal like Steve was probably more her type?

She was also wondering why she was bothering with all of this confusing analysis. She'd never been very analytical, and intuition—coupled with Adam's very precise schedule—told her that he'd be out of her life in a few very short weeks anyway.

Make that a few very long weeks, she corrected, feeling her heartbeat accelerate as the latch on the gate clanked open.

Keeping her head lowered over her task, she watched Adam's approach through the filter of her lashes. Within seconds his powerful strides covered the short distance and his equally powerful body was blocking the sun setting behind the palm trees. From her kneeling position on the lawn beside her walkway, she finally looked up.

"Do you play tennis?"

It was strictly intuitive, but she could swear that the flat tone he used to ask the totally out-of-the-blue question indicated that he wanted her to say no. "Yes," she returned with a touch of obstinacy, omitting the fact that she was lousy at it.

"I was afraid of that," he muttered under his breath.

"What?"

"I, ah..." As his voice trailed off he saw the yellow-green ball in the middle of her small front lawn. "I said I figured that because of all the tennis balls you've got around here," he concluded blandly. Actually, he'd been wondering if Stephanie was as interested in the sport as Diane was and had forgotten about the objects he nearly tripped on every time he came in to answer the phone. "You want to play tomorrow?"

"Tennis?"

"Yes, tennis," he mimicked, watching her eyes follow his descent as he sat down beside her. "We can play early in the morning before it gets too hot."

Pulling a chunk of crabgrass from the crack between the lawn and the walk, he tossed it onto her pile. He appeared every bit as comfortable with his offer as Stephanie felt uneasy. Her first inclination, right after she'd recovered from the fact that he'd asked, had actually been to accept the date. The voice of reason answered.

"I've got to take my car into the garage first thing, so I'm afraid I can't. Aren't you going to work out back in the morning? I thought your schedule..."

"Dino's not going anywhere. I thought I'd get to him after we got back from the courts. What time's your appointment?"

"I don't exactly have one. With as much business as I give them, the mechanics always squeeze me in."

The tiny lines feathering from the corners of his eyes deepened with his thoughtful frown. "If the thing gives you that much trouble, why don't you get a new one. I realize it would be an expense, but it would certainly be cheaper in the long run."

"I can't sell something I'm attached to," she stated in the same tone she would have used had he asked her to part with her left leg. The idea was ridiculous.

"Attached to? How can you be attached to a car?"

The erratic beat of her pulse was beginning to resume a more even pace. Adam always seemed a little less threatening when he was confused. "It's the only one I've ever owned. I paid for it myself, working for my dad on the weekends during college, and there's a lot of memories tied up in it. Sort of like an old scrapbook on wheels.''

"I see," he replied in a tone that clearly indicated he didn't.

Maybe if she put it in a more relevant context he'd understand. "Haven't you ever kept something just because it meant something to you?"

"Sure. My doctoral thesis and the artifacts and specimens I've—"

"Not like that," she cut in. "I mean things like a concert program, old letters, baseball cards. I'm pretty sure a boy wouldn't keep a boutonniere from a prom like a girl would keep her corsage, but that's the kind of thing I'm talking about."

"Why would you want to keep dead flowers? Or old letters for that matter. About all you could do with that stuff is put it in a box and store it somewhere."

Being a borderline pack rat, Stephanie couldn't really argue with that last statement. Her closets were full of "memories." Adam's were probably so neat it was scary.

It was apparent from the slight tilt of her head that she was pondering some way to make him understand how dead flowers could mean something. Having already decided that she was probably an incorrigible sentimentalist, he wasn't surprised to hear her finally say, "Sentimental value."

He could accept the explanation, though he couldn't fully appreciate it. Just because he put little stock in such things didn't mean he couldn't respect someone else's prerogative to do so. Proprietary interest he could understand, but how a person developed an emotional attachment to an inanimate object was beyond him.

Wondering if the key to her incomprehensible logic lay somewhere in an unfortunate past, he grasped the comment she'd made a moment ago. "You said you worked for your father. Did he make you work for him?"

A fleeting frown skipped across her face at his choice of words. It was quickly replaced with an easy smile. "Dad never tried to make me do anything. Neither did Mom. The knack they had for getting my sister and me to do the right thing had nothing to do with force. I can't explain how they did it, but I guess it just had something to do with acceptance and love."

For a moment Adam said nothing. His theory about her childhood was being thoroughly refuted by the genuine affection in her words. Maybe if he dug a little deeper. "You sound very close to your family."

Stephanie caught his strange, enigmatic glance. Though it was already gone by the time he leaned over to snatch the weed she was reaching for, something about it bothered her. She had the feeling she was being tested, yet there was nothing in his tone to indicate anything other than casual interest. "I am, even though we're spread out all over the state. Do you have family here? Any brothers or sisters?"

"I'm an only child," he returned, holding up a particularly healthy tangle of roots. "My mother and father are both retired anthropologists. Semiretired anyway. They've been in London for the past two years, working on a treatise for a university there. Scoot down. I just ran out of weeds."

As the sun sank a little lower and the stack of wilting vegetation beside them grew higher, their attention shifted from the things growing in the soil to some of the things Adam had found buried in it. His career, she discovered, had taken him from the Andes to the Aleutians, and his passion for the subject he taught was as intense as Stephanie's dedication to her own work.

Though her profession came with its own unique challenge, she kept the conversation centered on Adam. Not because she didn't want to talk about herself, but because the more she listened, the more clearly she could see the little boy he must have once been. Insatiably curious, always asking, "Why?" It was easy to see that there'd been more than teasing behind his remark about his being fascinated by puzzles—especially when he mentioned having come across something that made him rather curious about Dino. Even tempered as it was by maturity, the excitement in his eyes was quite evident.

Not knowing anything about paleontology, Stephanie couldn't appreciate the difference finding the hoofed foreleg had made. Since it was important to Adam, though, she found herself sharing his interest, even if she couldn't get terribly excited over the chunk of fossilized bone. Her curiosity as to Dino's identity never had been very acute. She really didn't care what it was as long as he got it out of her yard—which eventually reminded her that Adam wasn't doing what he'd stayed to do.

Drying her hands while Adam washed the chlorophyll stains from his at her kitchen sink, she smiled at the bright Hawaiian print shirt covering his back. To Stephanie, working in her yard was a labor of love. Adam regarded the chore as a nuisance he avoided by living in an apartment. Or, so he'd said. Whether he wanted to admit it or not, she knew he'd found the task rather relaxing.

"I don't think weeding my front yard was what you had in mind when you said you wanted to stay to get some work done."

Taking the towel she was holding out for him, he gave her a sideways glance. "I have been working." The towel was tossed on the counter a couple of seconds later, and

Adam stood smiling down at the top of her head. "On you."

With those two simple words, Adam managed to completely shatter the relaxed atmosphere. Marveling at how easily they'd talked, the teasing banter that had slipped between more serious topics, she'd forgotten to be wary. That sense of caution now sprang forth as forcefully as Athene had sprung from the head of almighty Zeus. Unlike Athene, the fabled mistress of strategy, Stephanie had no tactic to avoid the kind of danger Adam presented.

Putting physical distance between them seemed like the wisest course of action. Wise, but impossible. The way his eyes pinned hers as he grazed the line of her jaw with his knuckles kept her right where she was. Like a doe blinded by light, she could only stare into those unfathomable depths and wait for the moment when the hunter decided her fate.

"You don't play fair," Adam softly accused, seeing the vulnerability revealed in her upturned face. His mouth curved in the faintest of smiles. "The odd part about it, is that I don't think you're even into the games."

The constriction tightening her throat when his head lowered made it difficult to speak. The only attempt at protest she could manage was to weakly whisper, "Adam..."

"Hmm," he breathed against her temple, the faint vibration of his lips sending a pattern of tiny shocks to her brain.

What was she going to say? He'd said something about games, the games the other women in his life played no doubt. Something about that was supposed to bother her and, in a way, it did. It was hard to remember what that something was, though. How could she concentrate when his lips were moving against her skin like that? The feather-light path he was trailing along her brow, around the curve of her jaw and down her throat was making it absolutely impossible to think.

Easing his hands up her back, he drew her against him, his lips still working their mesmerizing magic. Any thought she might have had to concentrate on was sacrificed to sensation when he folded her to the hard breadth of his chest. Any attempt to move away was thwarted by the sudden longing awakened by the feel of his mouth closing insistently over hers.

The low moan filtering through the rushing in her ears seemed to come from somewhere deep in his chest. Another followed; her own when he pressed his palm to the side of her breast. Boldly he moved his thumb over her tightening nipple, the tip of his tongue darting into her mouth to capture her gasp.

The demands he'd so carefully withheld when he'd kissed her before were now being issued quite clearly. His tongue pushed past the tentative stirrings of her own as he aligned her soft curves more intimately to his body. Caressing, coaxing, he lead her to answer each thrust and parry, hungrily accepting her surrender as something he had a right to expect.

Her hands were braced against his shoulders. Needing to feel the solid strength draining her own, she splayed her fingers across the broad band of muscle straining beneath his shirt. When her hand slid down his sides and around his back, she felt, rather than heard, his quick intake of breath. The controlled urgency she sensed in him found its counterpart in her.

She didn't want to acknowledge how rapidly her feelings for him were changing. She wanted to go on ignoring that sense of the inevitable assailing her every waking moment. But ignoring something wouldn't make it go away, and abandoning her attempts at denial would leave her helpless.

What defenses she had were rapidly crumbling beneath his caresses. The things he was doing to her, the feel of his hands, his lips, were creating a heat so intense that the only form of escape seemed to be in that same sensual inferno. If she gave herself up to it, she wouldn't have to fight it anymore.

Stephanie never did give up easily.

Just as she was about to pull back, she felt Adam's arms slip away and his hands settle on her shoulders. "This isn't going to work," he said raggedly, totally mystifying her. Using his index finger to smooth the wisps of hair from her flushed cheek, he tucked the errant strands behind her ear.

He was obviously referring to them in some way, but she needed to hear the context. It was one thing for her to know it couldn't ever work between them, but having him say it left her with a feeling she didn't like at all. "What isn't?" she asked, willing the trembling in her body to cease. It was a feat she couldn't quite manage.

"Forget it," he mumbled, offering her something that might have looked like a smile if it hadn't been for the desire still darkening his features. "I was talking to myself."

"Is that something you do often?"

His finger moved over her slightly swollen lips. "It's an affliction I seemed to have picked up recently." He liked the idea of having left her looking well kissed, but she wouldn't like the idea of knowing that he'd approached the kiss with the intent of finding out what there was about the feel of her that was so different from the other women he'd known. That intent had vaporized within a split second, and he'd been even more bewildered than before at how swiftly he responded to her. It was that same burning he could still feel in his loins that made him quietly voice the thought that seemed to be constantly on his mind.

"Do you have any idea how badly I want to make love to you right now?" Seeing the color return to her cheeks as she lowered her head, he nudged her chin back up. "It's okay, Stephanie. I'm not in the habit of taking something that isn't offered, and I know all about cold showers. But you are offering me something I don't think I want to turn my back on just yet. I haven't figured out what it is, but I'm working on it." After brushing his lips across hers, he tapped the end of her nose with his finger and strolled over to the back door. "Since you can't play tennis tomorrow, let's try next Tuesday."

"Adam. Come back here! I'm not..." The click of the door closing after him quite effectively cut her off.

Her new ivory curtains, the ones she'd hung on the window of her back door this morning, were still swaying from Adam's departure when she jerked the door open.

Five

Adam had one hand stuffed in the pocket of his white tennis shorts to hold his racket under his arm. His other hand was on the door he'd just pushed open. "What do you mean, you don't know how to keep score?"

"Just what I said." Stephanie gave him a bland smile. "I tried to tell you I'm not very good at this."

Preceding him through the doors from the Humanities Building, where her Tuesday mythology class had just been dismissed, she put on her large, rose-tinted sunglasses and dropped her glass case into the tote bag slung over her shoulder. Along with her books and wallet, the closest thing she owned to a tennis outfit was stuffed in there; a white T-shirt and shorts and a pair of light blue Nikes with chewed-up laces. Adam had said she could change in the P.E. Building.

The two young women jogging toward them as they cut across the crowded walkway looked like they'd just come from there. "Hi, Dr. Colter," the one in the fuchsia track suit greeted. The one wearing the sweats with UCLA stamped on the chest gave him a broad smile.

"Ladies," he returned with a preoccupied nod.

Amazing, Stephanie thought as the coeds passed. He didn't even notice the exceptional balance it took for the girls to continue their forward motion with their necks cranked around like that. It was clear enough to her that it wasn't the sight of a professor wandering around campus in tennis clothes that held their attention. The California-casual atmosphere was quite prevalent here during summer term. It was obviously this particular professor's physical assets that were appreciated by the female student population. She couldn't help wondering if there was a waiting list for the classes he taught.

"I know you said you were lousy," Adam was saying while she hurried to keep up with him, "but I thought you were just using that as another excuse. I didn't know you were serious."

It wasn't any wonder he hadn't listened to her. After having tried every argument she could think of not to accept the date, every one of which he'd ignored, coming up with something like an inability to play the sport hadn't been particularly effective. Especially since halfway through that "discussion" she'd suddenly found herself very much wanting to do what she'd kept insisting she didn't.

"The only part I really have trouble with is my serve. Well, that and keeping score. I never could understand why one point equalled ten. Or, is it fifteen?"

"Fifteen. Tell you what. I'll find a bucket of balls and we'll practice your serve for a while before we get started."

"It won't do any good. I've taken three sets of beginners' lessons and every..."

A teasing smile preceded his interruption. "Haven't you learned by now that arguing with me won't get you anywhere?"

"Isn't that the truth," she muttered while watching him extract a set of keys from his pocket as they approached the outer door leading to the faculty locker room. What he did for a pair of jeans was nothing compared to what his body accomplished for those shorts.

Deliberately pulling her eyes from his back, and his backside, she followed his direction to the women's dressing room while he went off in search of the tennis balls. Arguing with Adam about anything was an exercise in futility. It wasn't that he always had to be right. It was just that, unless she could back up her opinion with something concrete, he couldn't see her side at all. Or, could he, and he was just being his slightly exasperating self by pretending otherwise? There were times when she could swear he enjoyed baiting her just to see what kind of a reaction he'd get.

A soft smile touched her lips as, stepping back out into the bright sunlight after she'd changed, she saw Adam heading toward the court where he'd said he'd meet her. If she had anything to say about it, he'd never know the intensity of the reactions he provoked.

The smile faded. Something kept telling her she might not have any say in the matter. It was as if some power beyond her was making the decisions where he was concerned.

It was only a fleeting thought, one she immediately dismissed as horrifying, but was it possible that she might be falling in...?

"Love," Adam was explaining an hour later, "equals zero. So thirty-love means one side has thirty points, or the equivalent of two, and the other, nothing. Understand?"

"About as well as I'm going to." It wasn't just the exertion that made her response sound a little breathless. It was the way Adam was pressed to her back, his breath fanning the wisps of hair at her temple as he spoke.

"Good. Now, let's try your serve again. Drop down in back." With his hand folded around her wrist he stepped away to guide her racket down. "That's it. Now, toss the ball and—" something between a chuckle and a groan preceded his laconic "—let's try it again. You've almost got it."

"Let's not," she suggested, wiping the perspiration from her forehead with the back of her hand. "My arm feels like it's ready to fall off."

"Giving up already?" he teased.

"Absolutely."

"But we haven't even played yet."

A smile danced in her eyes when she met the more subtle one in his. "Pouting is conduct unbecoming a professor, Adam. If you want to *play* tennis instead of giving lessons, you'll have to find another partner."

The sun caught the threads of pale gold woven through his breeze-tossed hair as his head lowered slightly. Touching the tiny drop of moisture beaded at the base of her throat, he let his finger trail down to meet the scooped neck of her T-shirt. "What if I don't want to play with anyone else? What if I said I'm glad you aren't Ms. Superjock and that I like the idea of being able to teach you something a professional instructor couldn't? You've got the ability. It's just your concentration that needs work."

From behind the protection of her sunglasses, she blinked up at him. Didn't he know that *he* was the reason she couldn't keep her mind on what she was supposed to be doing? It was a source of astonishment to her that she'd been able to do as well as she had.

He knows, she thought wryly when he gave her a devilish grin. No man was *that* dense.

"Of course," he continued, letting his hand drift away to pry her racket from her fingers. "I could just give up on you I guess. Anybody who studies mythology really is a hopeless cause, you know."

His teasing was becoming quite familiar. So was the enervating warmth she felt at his smile. The flush of heat she'd felt when his finger had dipped dangerously close to her breast was something she preferred not to think about. "I really wish you'd stop picking on my class," she muttered, not really meaning it. Discussing her favorite subject with a skeptic was quite stimulating, actually. "On the other hand, I should probably be grateful that you weren't around last year. You'd have had a field day with mysticism and the occult."

He slowly arched one eyebrow. "Mysticism and the occult? You mean black magic and voodoo and all that?"

"Uh-huh. I had a student at the high school who'd gotten caught up in it. She was a very bright kid, and her influence with some of the other students was incredible. I studied it so I'd know what we were up against."

"Ah . . . you don't believe in witchcraft, do you?"

There was so much caution in his question that it was all Stephanie could do to keep from laughing. "No, Adam," she assured him, smiling openly at his relief. "But I do believe that the human mind can create its own kind of power. Psychologically we're capable of undermining ourselves to such an extreme that thinking something bad is going to happen is enough to make it happen. The other side of that phenomenon is the power of positive thinking. You know that maxim, 'You are what you eat'?''

Obviously not sure where this conversation was leading, Adam just nodded.

''Well,'' she continued easily, ''the flip side of that is 'you are what you believe.' ''

''Does that make you a myth?''

''What?''

''You believe in myths. So based on your hypothesis, that must be what you are. A figment of someone's imagination.''

She was fairly certain of it now, and by the time she'd collected her things and Adam had led her to his car, she was absolutely convinced that she was right. Adam was deliberately being obtuse.

Attempting to explain how her interest in the myths wasn't based on belief so much as not disbelief wasn't working at all. Adam kept insisting that merely accepting a possibility wasn't enough. ''Simply put,'' he stated in a very professorial tone as he switched on the ignition, ''there is a fallacy in your argument because it offers nothing tangible.''

''What about something like love then,'' she countered offhandedly, mentally holding her breath. ''That's not tangible, but a lot of people believe in it.''

His quiet chuckle seemed to relax his compelling features even more. ''When someone comes up with an equation for an emotion, I'd like to see it. So far, I don't think anyone has.'' A quick glance was tossed toward the rearview mirror as he prepared to back out of the parking space. "I need to grab a change of clothes. Mind if we stop by my apartment?"

Since he was concentrating on the car behind them, waiting for it to pass, he didn't see her mouth tighten when she quietly replied no.

Whether he knew it or not, he'd answered the question she hadn't quite asked. Love wasn't explicable. Therefore, it looked very much like Adam Colter didn't believe that such a thing existed.

Adam was faced with the last half of that same thought a few hours later, though in a very different context.

After working alone all afternoon, he'd found what he'd been looking for. Parts of it, that is. The satisfaction he always felt when a fragment was discovered had grown with each bit of dirt he'd carefully dusted away. But that exciting sense of accomplishment had slowly been replaced with consternation as more and more of the fossil revealed itself.

He knew that what he was seeing couldn't possibly be. There was nothing extraordinary about the smooth pieces of skull lying exactly where he had uncovered them. And though almost half of the skull was still missing, the largest portion was definitely a complete frontal lobe. It was what was protruding from its center that Adam had been staring at for the last several minutes—the long, spiraled horn that bore a remarkable resemblance to the one depicted on the poster Stephanie had hanging above her table.

"Coincidence," he muttered to himself, dismissing the comparison when he heard Stephanie calling him.

Stephanie couldn't see Adam at all. Knowing he was probably on his knees in the hole, she called across the empty yard. "Adam? Dave's on the phone." Surprisingly enough, this was the only call Adam had received today. In fact, it was the only one he'd received since last Friday. All of his girlfriends must have taken a vacation. "Adam? Are you down there?"

From the preoccupation she heard in the voice coming from the hole, she knew her question hadn't registered. "Come down here, will you? I need you to take a look at something."

"What about your call?"

"Ask if I can call him back."

A few moments later, Stephanie stood hesitantly in the middle of her torn-up lawn. Adam had said he wanted her to look at something. Since whatever it was was probably the thing she'd avoided looking at so far, the prospect wasn't particularly appealing, "He said you were quite capable of calling him back if it was your ability you were questioning. If you were asking if you *may* call him back, he said yes. It's not anything that won't wait."

Dr. David Abrahms was certifiably brilliant—which probably fed his occasional penchant for absolute correctness. Adam dismissed what he considered the irrelevant parts of the message and slowly walked around the curious specimen still lying in the dirt. His fingers itched to pick it up, but he didn't. It was imperative that everything remain in its exact position until photos could be taken when the dig was completed. Discoveries had to be substantiated. If this was what it looked like it was, he'd need all the documentation he could get.

Maybe his perspective was wrong. Maybe that horn wasn't centered quite as perfectly as it seemed to be. Maybe it was just the position of the sun that made it appear to have those odd colors. "There's a pair of calipers on the patio table," he called to the top of Stephanie's head, the only part of her visible from his position several feet down. "Bring them with you, will you?"

Stephanie had no idea what calipers looked like, but by simple deduction she figured out that what he wanted was the scissorlike object lying next to a trowel. Not a difficult accomplishment, since the only other item on the table was a notepad.

Instrument in hand, she positioned herself at the top of the plank serving as a walkway into the hole. "Here," she said, keeping her eyes fixed on the patched section of her back fence.

Adam squinted up at her, shielding his eyes from the late-afternoon sun to let them travel over the mauve terry-cloth romper she was wearing. It didn't have any straps and the bottom of the shorts was just brief enough to do full justice to her legs. A full five seconds passed before he remembered what it was that he'd wanted. "You can't see this from there."

"I know. That's why I'm staying right where I am. If you want these things, come and get them."

"Oh, come on, Stephanie."

"I don't like dead things, Adam."

"It's not going to do anything to you."

That was true...probably. But everyone was entitled to a few aversions, and this just happened to be one of hers. She did feel a little childish, though, standing there thinking about putting her hand over her eyes. After all, she was a grown woman and she knew it was impossible for the thing to suddenly spring to life.

"Nothing's going to happen," Adam said, as if reading her mind. "Trust me, okay?"

Famous last words, she drawled to herself. Then, taking a deep breath she started down the three-foot-wide board. She didn't release that breath until she was standing behind Adam—who immediately stepped to the side.

The revulsion she'd expected wasn't there. The skeleton, the left side of its rib cage still buried, was nothing at all like the gruesome collection of bones her vivid imagination had constructed. Smooth and gray, the fossil looked more like stone than anything else—except for the beautifully colored, perfectly spiraled length lying several feet from the rest of it.

"My God," she whispered, immediately recognizing the unique coloration of the horn. "Dino's a unicorn!"

"That's absurd, Stephanie." Taking the calipers, he knelt down, measuring the position of the horn where it was attached to the lobe. "Damn."

"What's the matter?"

"It's centered."

"If you mean it's in the middle of his head, of course it is."

"I meant it's centered on this portion of the skull, which," he admitted, "happens to be its forehead. Most of the anterior portion is still missing, and until I find the rest of it, there's no way I'm going to start drawing conclusions . . . let alone jumping to them." He didn't look quite as positive as he sounded. "There's probably another horn around here somewhere."

"If that horn is in the middle of his forehead, where would the other one have grown from? Behind his ear?"

With a touch of teasing arrogance, the conviction that had been missing a moment ago surfaced. "It can't be a unicorn, Stephanie."

"Why not? There's lots of evidence that they were real."

"Legends aren't evidence," he dryly informed her. "Scientifically, there's no basis for the assumption that this is anything other than..." Cutting himself off, he ran his fingers through his hair, revealing the furrowed lines in his brow.

"Than what?" she prodded when several seconds had passed and he still hadn't completed his statement.

"I'm not sure yet." The reluctant concession was quickly amended with scholarly certainty. "I do know what it isn't. Elimination being an accepted form of eventual identification, I can safely begin by eliminating mythical beasts from the possibilities of choice."

There were times when his irritating insistence on proof seemed like nothing but plain old stubbornness. She preferred to think of her own stubborn streak as being the courage of her convictions.

Not about to be put off by his reasoning, she decided to fight logic with logic, or a reasonable facsimile thereof. She'd accumulated quite a list of "facts" over the years. "Even a scientist can't disregard recorded history," she prefaced in the same pedantic tone he'd used. "Back in 400 B.C., Ctesias quite accurately described a deerlike animal with a long horn whose tip was red, the middle black and the base white. Dino's about the same size of a deer, so how do you explain the fact that his horn looks exactly like that?"

"Who the devil is Ctesias?"

Pleased with the credentials she was about to offer, she did her best not to look as if she was about to win a point. She would accept her victory graciously. "A very respected Greek historian and physician."

"Never heard of him."

Undaunted by Adam's dismissal of the one prominent authority she was using to support her argument, and momentarily forgetting that he hadn't answered her question, she pressed on. There was one authority he had to acknowledge. "Then, what about the Bible? The word 'unicorn' appeared quite often in early versions. Eventually it was translated as 'wild ox,' but it referred to the same animal that was incorporated into icons of the Virgin Mary and Christ as symbols of purity."

Adam was shaking his head. "I've never studied theology, but I'm sure there's quite a few people who'd take exception to that particular translation. I also never said there wasn't the *belief* that unicorns existed. My point is that there's never been any proof."

"What do you call that then?" she challenged, pointing at the object beside his foot.

"Keratin."

"In English, Adam. And you know that whatever it was you said wasn't what I meant."

Still avoiding committing himself by saying anything she might think was agreement, he simply muttered, "Same stuff as fingernails," then frowned at her. "Do you have any big pieces of plastic?"

"Are you trying to change the subject?"

"No," he said blandly. "I'm trying to figure out a way to cover this up."

"Why?"

"To protect it." And to keep anybody else from seeing it, he added to himself.

"Oh. Well, I've got part of a roll of the black plastic I use in the flower beds. Will that work?"

"That'll do just fine. Now, where were we?"

"You were in the process of evading my question," she reminded him, unconsciously locking her knees. She wasn't going to let him divert her with that darn dimple of his.

Well, maybe he could divert her a little, she thought, acknowledging a tiny thrill of anticipation when he continued to smile down at her. There was something about arguing with Adam that was rather stimulating. As incongruous as it seemed, the heady tension she felt whenever she was around him always increased when they were disagreeing. It made absolutely no sense at all.

"I wasn't trying to avoid an answer. It's just that, right now, I don't have one. The one thing I am certain of, though, is that there's a reasonable explanation for all of this."

"Meaning you refuse to admit that it *could* be a unicorn?"

"Don't go getting all defensive," he chided, looking very much like he was enjoying making her that way. "If you want to get literal about it, at the moment, this *is* a one-horned animal, which is all 'unicorn' means."

The way his mouth twitched to suppress his smile told her that he wasn't taking any of this seriously. Willing herself to indulge him for the moment, she waited for him to continue. He didn't have to explain the meaning of the word to her. She knew enough Greek to understand that "uni" meant "one" and "corn" was "horn."

"Remember the goat that circus billed as a unicorn last year. The one where someone had surgically moved the horn buds to..."

"We're not talking about publicity hype," she interrupted in quiet exasperation. "We're talking about something that existed thousands of years ago."

"We don't know that it existed. Stephanie, I've been in this field for a long time, and I'm the first to admit that I've still got a lot to learn, but I've yet to come across a phenomenon that couldn't be defined eventually. It's just a little unusual to happen onto two at the same time."

He seemed so blasted sure of himself, but there was no way she was going to rule out the possibility of there actually having been such a creature. "Anything's possible," she proclaimed reasonably, "even if it might appear a little improbable. Not everything has to be explained so we can understand it, you know." The satisfaction she felt with her reasoning lasted all of a second and a half. "What do you mean, 'two at the same time'?"

"I was wondering if you were going to catch that."

The amusement she'd seen slip into his eyes while he studied her animated expression was slowly turning to something quite unfamiliar. It was an almost predatory gleam that didn't coincide at all with the casualness in his deep voice. "One," he said, taking the step that put him squarely in front of her, "is Dino."

Looking straight ahead, all she could see was a line of golden brown hair and tanned chest between the open front of his shirt. She tipped her head back. "The other?"

For a moment he said nothing. He just stood there, his eyes moving slowly over her still features. When he spoke, his gaze had settled on the soft part of her mouth. "You."

That one word, said on a half whisper, was a verbal caress so gentle she could almost feel it wrapping around her. Stunned by the impact of his simple response, she could only stare up at the darkening blue of his eyes and wonder at his meaning. He thought of her as something unusual?

"I'm just me," she tried to defend, and saw him smile.

"Oh, Stephanie," he breathed, cupping her face between his hands. "You have no idea of all the things you are."

The kiss she'd been aching for all day was feathered over her mouth. Seconds passed, but he didn't deepen it the way she wanted. When she started to lean toward him, to create the contact he was deliberately withholding, he lifted his head.

Confused, she blinked up at him, and the breath she'd just inhaled locked in her lungs.

His hands drifted to her waist, drawing her forward, then moved up until his palms pressed lightly against the sides of her breasts. Never allowing his gaze to waver from her eyes, he slipped his thumb over her nipple, teasing the hard little bud with a slow, circular motion.

"No," he said, when her head lowered to break the mesmerizing contact of his eyes. "Look at me. I want you to know what it does to me when I feel you respond like this."

Little shocks radiated inward as he continued the incredibly light caress. They were abruptly magnified by the feel of his body arching just enough for him to press himself against her pelvic bone. His eyes remained steady on hers, the desire clearly defined in their depths as apparent as his recognition of her own.

"Adam." She'd barely whispered his name when she felt the gentle pressure of his mouth on hers. From the soft way he was kissing her, his lips full and firm against her own, he must have known that she had meant his name as an invitation. Allowing one hand to slip around her back, he pressed the other more firmly to her breast.

She leaned toward him to curve her arms around his neck, her fingers grazing lightly over his skin before pushing through the silky texture of his hair. There were so many ways they differed from each other, yet the only ones she could recall at the moment were how small his large frame made her feel, how hard and solid his muscles felt against her softer curves. It seemed that there were some other differences she should be considering, but she couldn't remember them. She could only think of how much she wanted this, and how right it felt to be in his arms.

The tiny, nipping kisses he began to string across her throat were leaving a trail of heat along her bare shoulder. "So soft," he murmured against her skin. With one finger he edged the elastic of her romper down a bit, his tongue touching the hollow between her breasts. "So incredibly soft. I need to touch you, Stephanie. Let me."

When what he was about to do slowly registered, she closed her fingers over his hand. Willing the sensual fog enshrouding her to lift, she drew a trembling breath. "We're outside," she said, knowing the statement sounded rather ridiculous. Adam knew quite well where they were. "Someone might . . ."

"No one can see us down here. We're in an eight-foot hole and your fence is five feet high. I just want to touch you, to feel you." His lips hovered over hers. "There's a few other things I'd like to do, but I'll settle for that for now. I won't rush you, sweetheart, I promise." A chain of deliriously sensual kisses were strung from the corner of her mouth to her temple, her throat, and the top of her romper was being slowly lowered to her waist.

Later she could wonder why she didn't try to stop him, but not now. It seemed she had no will of her own, only a need that had no definition. That need grew stronger as his hands closed over the soft swells of her breasts, and she heard the low moan coming from deep within his chest. The flick of his tongue against one peaked nipple sent a jolt of pure fire racing madly through her midsection. The gentle suckling motion of his mouth when it

...be tempted!

**See inside for special
4 FREE BOOKS offer**

Silhouette Desire®

Discover deliciously different Romance with 4 Free Novels from

Silhouette ❤ Desire®

...be enchanted!

As a Silhouette home subscriber, the enchantment begins with Elaine Camp's HOOK, LINE AND SINKER, the story of a woman who must overcome a lie to make real romance possible...Diane Palmer's LOVE BY PROXY, her startling beauty convinced him she was the woman he wanted—on his own terms...Joan Hohl's A MUCH NEEDED HOLIDAY, what begins as a contest of wills turns into an all-consuming passion Kate cannot seem to control...and Laurel Evans' MOONLIGHT SERENADE, the story of a woman who enjoyed her life in the slow lane —until she met the handsome New York TV producer.

...be our guest!

These exciting, love-filled, full-length novels are yours *absolutely FREE along with your Folding Umbrella and Mystery Gift*...a present from us to you. They're yours to keep no matter what you decide.

...be delighted!

After you receive your 4 FREE books, we'll send you 6 more Silhouette Desire novels each and every month to examine FREE for 15 days. If you decide to keep them, pay just $11.70 (a $13.50 value)— with no additional charges for home delivery! If you aren't completely delighted, just drop us a note and we'll cancel your subscription, no questions asked.

EXTRA BONUS: You'll also receive the Silhouette Books Newsletter FREE with each book shipment. Every issue is filled with interviews, news about upcoming books, recipes from your favorite authors, and more.

To get your 4 FREE novels, Folding Umbrella, and Mystery Gift, just fill out and mail the attached order card. Remember, the first 4 novels and both gifts are yours to keep. Are you ready to be tempted?

closed over the bud created wave after wave of that same heat.

She eased her hands from his shoulders, moving them over the rigid cords in his neck. Closing her eyes, she pressed his head to her, encouraging the tension she could feel building within him. She needed for him to touch her like this. She'd needed it forever.

Adam must have sensed the moment when her legs decided they weren't going to support her any longer. Keeping one arm around her back, he lifted his head and pulled open the front of his shirt. The combined effect of his bare skin against hers and his tongue demanding entrance into her mouth threatened to deplete the last vestiges of her strength.

Time and place became irrelevant. She had no idea how long they stood there, wrapped in each others arms. The only certainty was the ragged edge she heard in the question he finally murmured against her temple. "What have you done to me, Stephanie?"

"I was just wondering the same thing myself... about you." Her voice was no steadier than his. "Do you have much more to do out here?"

"No," he replied, unable to keep the expectancy from his tone. Stroking her hair, he added a husky, "Why?"

The breath she drew filled her lungs with the masculine scent of perspiration and spicy after-shave. The effect was doing nothing to slow the rapid pounding of her heart. Neither was the feel of his chest, hard and warm against her breasts.

It took more strength of will than she knew she possessed to pull back from him just then. She only moved far enough away to see his face, though. "Because if you're through, I'd better go get the plastic so you can cover Dino up."

The desire darkening his eyes was now shadowed with disappointment. Obviously the reason for her question was not the one he'd wanted to hear. After a moment's hesitation he offered her a smile that didn't quite work. "Good idea."

There was a definite amount of reluctance in the way he reached between them to lift her top up and let her step from his embrace. A telling huskiness remained in his voice when he called to her as she turned away. "Mind if I use some of the rocks up there by the fence?"

Assuring him that she didn't, and too busy grappling with the enormity of what was happening between them to concern herself with why he'd want them, she hurried up the plank. She wasn't running. Deep inside it felt as if she was though. And it felt like she was running toward something, rather than from it.

She deliberately slowed her pace as she approached the garage door. It was quite possible that she was getting concerned over nothing—if the loss of one's mind could be considered an inconsequential occurrence. No sane person would play with fire, and that's exactly what she'd been doing.

Apollo and a unicorn. What was happening to her sense of reality anyway?

That question answered itself a few minutes later. Adam found her in the garage, struggling with the heavy roll of plastic jammed among her gardening supplies. "I'll get it," he said, the tension in his voice visible in the tight set of his jaw. A moment later, he walked out, leaving her with her arms hugging her stomach.

Reality was the quivering sensation knotting her insides, and the very mortal male who had caused it.

It wasn't until Adam had secured the heavy black material with some of the rocks Stephanie's pool contractor had left piled by the fence that he finally allowed himself to knock on her back door. More than once, he'd abandoned his task to start up the plank, only to find himself heading right down it again. He'd been feeling a lot of things in the past twenty minutes that were quite unfamiliar, indecision being one of them.

The volume of the stereo had grown louder as he'd crossed the patio. It reached its crescendo when the door swung in. "I'd like to call Dave back," he announced over the booming instrumentation. "Can I use your phone?"

He couldn't help but notice that Stephanie's eyes didn't quite meet his. With a small shrug, she mumbled, "Sure," and squatted to catch the puppy racing for the open door.

Zeus landed in her lap a second later, greeting Adam with his usual growl.

Damn dog, he muttered to himself, not at all sure why he was suddenly in such a foul temper. Punching out Dave's number, he leaned against the counter. His eyes followed Stephanie's every move as she walked into the living room, cooing to the blissfully panting mongrel in her arms.

The line was busy. That only added to Adam's frustration.

And he was frustrated. With himself, and with Stephanie. The physical aspects of that particular manifestation weren't all that comfortable, either.

He almost wished she'd stopped him before he'd had a chance to actually feel her incredible softness. All he'd wanted to do was touch her, but when he'd felt her melting against him, he knew he could never be satisfied with anything less than everything. Then he'd seen the flicker of feminine fear in the ebony darkness of her eyes. Even with her desire so evident, it had been unmistakable. That was probably the only reason he'd let her go instead of carrying her off to her bedroom. He didn't want her to be afraid of him.

She was still afraid of him. At least he thought so when she emerged from the living room with her arms crossed beneath her breasts. There seemed to be a fair amount of wariness shadowing the tentative smile she was directing at his chin.

Six

It wasn't just fear that made Stephanie stay on the opposite side of the room. It was also a case of not trusting herself to move closer. The remembered feel of his hard body pressed so intimately to hers simply wouldn't go away. Decreasing the amount of space separating them would only increase that enervating tension.

"Wasn't Dave home?" she inquired, grasping the most obvious way to break the momentary silence.

"Line was busy."

"Oh."

Adam's eyes shifted from her to the phone, then back. "I'll try him again in a minute."

There didn't seem to be anything to say to that, so she just gave him a perfunctory nod.

Several more seconds ticked by. Then, Adam straightened up. He didn't move from his spot, though, careful to leave her the ten feet of space she was allowing herself. "It's after six. You hungry?" he asked.

"Not really. I could fix something for you if you are... hungry, I mean."

She couldn't tell if he was contemplating her offer or the extent of his appetite while he stood there staring at her bare feet. By the time he mumbled, "That's okay," his eyes had taken a very thorough journey up her calves to her thighs.

Her heart rate, already noticeably erratic, doubled its pace. The only visible effect of that unveiled inspection was the tightening of her fingers around her upper arms while she struggled to find something innocuous to say. "You sure?" she finally asked, lacking a more brilliant comment.

"Yes."

Now what? They couldn't just stand here staring at each other.

None of the silences they'd shared before had been quite so stressful as the intermittent ones filling the stiff bits of conversation now. What wasn't being said was definitely affecting the strained attempts to break the increasingly electric atmosphere. The faint strains of Johnny Mathis softly crooning the chorus to "Hello Young Lovers" wasn't helping much, either. She should have either turned the stereo all the way off or left it at its usual semiblare.

Adam must have thought so, too. Stepping to the sink, he grabbed the bar of soap. All that could be heard now was the sound of rushing water as he scrubbed the dirt from his hands and the hasty clearing of his throat. "By the way, thanks for the plastic."

Mumbling a quiet "Sure" to his back, she latched on to the diversionary subject. "Why did you cover Dino up anyway? The kids will just have to uncover him when they get here tomorrow.''

"They won't be coming tomorrow." He turned the water off and reached for the towel looped through the refrigerator door. "I've decided not to hold my class here anymore."

Before she could even begin to start analyzing the reasons for the distinct sinking feeling in the pit of her stomach, Adam was moving closer. Still drying his hands, he tossed an absent frown toward the poster of the unicorn scampering through a field of flowers.

"Except for Dave, I don't want anybody around Dino until I've had a chance to dig around on my own. Think I'll ask him to come over and take a look at what we've got."

More relieved than she cared to admit by that explanation, she slowly released the breath she'd been holding—only to find the next one getting stuck again. Adam's eyes had fastened on the cleavage visible above the mauve terry cloth. His mouth parted slightly, and the knot in her stomach tightened when she saw the tip of his tongue touch the edge of his upper lip.

Slowly he raised his eyes to hers. "Stephanie," he began, then hesitated as if he'd changed his mind about whatever he was going to say. Looking down at the towel he was holding, he laid it on the counter. "I think I'd better go."

"No."

The word was a soft expulsion of breath, an unconscious reaction to his unexpected pronouncement.

"What did you say?"

"I said no," she repeated softly, and saw something dark and intense flare in the deep blue of his eyes.

The sensual awareness sparking between them was so strong that it acted like a magnet, drawing her toward him. Unable to fight its pull, no longer wanting to, she touched the rigid line of his jaw with the tips of her fingers. "I don't want you to leave."

A surge of doubt stilled her hand, and she let it fall to her side. Except for the quick breath he'd drawn, Adam hadn't moved.

Her head lowered. Adam's finger under her chin tipped it back up. "I don't want to, either, but we're both thinking about what happened a while ago, and trying to make small talk isn't going to make either one of us forget about it. You know what's going to happen if I stay, Stephanie. And, God help me, walking away from you right now is going to be the hardest thing I've ever done in my life."

It wouldn't have mattered if she'd found the courage to beg him not to go. No sound could possibly have gotten past the constriction in her throat. He was telling her that he wanted her, yet he wasn't going to ask anything of her that she wasn't prepared to give. In his own way, he was saying that she mattered to him—that he cared.

The words weren't necessary. Though she said nothing, her eloquent eyes were speaking quite clearly.

Adam was staring down at her, looking very much like he was just beginning to comprehend some very elemental truth. "You're not going to let me walk away, are you?"

The quiet flatness in his tone made the question sound like an indisputable statement—one he was already confirming when she finally started to form the words her heart had found.

"This morning when I said you must be a myth because of all the crazy things you believe, I didn't realize how close I'd come to discovering why I've never been able to figure you out. Maybe that is what you are. You're really Aphrodite and, as in the legend, simply by speaking your name I've fallen under your spell." He seemed disconcerted with his own irrationality, yet oddly accepting. "How could a mere mortal ever hope to understand a goddess?"

Her? A goddess? Bemused by the poetry in his words, trembling at the sureness of his touch when his fingers settled on her bare shoulders to pull her closer, she smiled. "You don't believe in myths, remember?"

"I'm not sure what I believe right now," he admitted huskily. "My rational mind knows it's impossible, but there's no other way I can explain what you've done to me . . . why I need you so badly that I can't seem to think of anything else." His voice lowered in gentle command. "Tell me what you want, Stephanie."

Until now she hadn't really formed the words in her mind. What she wanted had just seemed to exist in some nebulous form that seemed safer if it wasn't put into more concrete terms. Adam was waiting, though, leaving the choice up to her.

There was no decision to make; the Fates had already decided the outcome.

The beat of his heart felt strong and a little unsteady when she laid her hand on his chest. "I want you, Adam."

She wasn't sure if she'd moved forward or if Adam had pulled her against him. It didn't matter. What did was the feel of his mouth moving over hers and the heady knowledge that he wanted her as desperately as she did him.

Aphrodite. To think that he had compared her to the goddess of love was enough to embolden the caresses she was stroking along his back. The smoothness of his skin sensitized her fingers as she explored the ridge of muscles running parallel to the indentation of his spine. When she reached the low-slung waist of his jeans, she felt a spasm shudder through him. An instant later, he was seeking entrance into the sweet darkness of her mouth.

She welcomed that intrusion. Imitating each stroke of his tongue, she sought to break the iron control that kept his hands from moving up to find the softness she was pressing to his chest. His fingers were splayed around her rib cage, his thumbs tantalizing the firm undersides of her breasts.

The groan coming from deep inside him was followed by the gentling of his kiss. With that decrease in pressure, she could feel his lips trembling slightly as he moved them first to one corner of her mouth and then to the other. "Where's Zeus?" he asked, tightening his arm around her back while he rained a series of moist nips from the base of her throat to her temple.

It took a moment before the strained words made any sense. Curving her arms around his neck, she mumbled, "In his playpen."

She was about to ask why he wanted to know, when she heard him mutter, "Good," and felt him bend to lift her in his arms. Her question was immediately forgotten. Adam's long, steady strides were carrying them down the hall.

The warmth of his mouth closing over hers blotted out the flicker of hesitation she felt when he lowered her to her ivory-eyelet-draped canopy bed. The tenderness in his eyes when, long seconds later, he pulled back to slip the romper from her body spoke of a need beyond physical desire. It was the unexpected hint of vulnerability softening the chiseled set of his features that twisted so forcefully around her heart.

She lay there before him, clad only in filmy pink bikinis. Never had she felt so shy, or so wanton.

His eyes stroked her with such heat she could almost feel the path they were burning over her. Not once did his gaze waver as he tossed his shirt to the floor and worked loose the buckle of his belt and the snap of his jeans. The slow scrape of the metal zipper seemed to echo in her ears.

Then, he was kicking aside his jeans to strip away his shorts, and he was standing beside the bed. Proudly, magnificently male, he loomed over her, drinking in the sight before him. Her smile was tentative, her arms trembling as she raised them in silent invitation.

From the moment he stretched out beside her, nothing seemed quite real. The huge canopy bed became a lacy cocoon of warmth when he folded her to him, adoring her with his lips, his hands. The muted cry of the birds calling to their mates from the orange tree outside her window became the melodious tones of a lyre when she answered the heated demands in his kiss. He made her feel like a goddess. Cherished and precious. And he was her Apollo. Powerful, gentle, reckless and wise.

His fingers played over her shoulders, her back, then cupped the firm flesh of her hips to press her to his hardness. The liquid fire in her veins seemed to center at that point of contact, and she instinctively arched against him.

"Adam," she whispered.

"In a while," he breathed against her seeking lips. "I want you to be as ready as I am. There's no way I'll be able to hold back once I'm inside you."

The boldness of his words inflamed her as much as the sweet torture he inflicted on her breast when his mouth closed firmly over the tight bud. His tongue circled slowly, teasing, coaxing, before he started to suckle so gently she could feel each pull transmitting itself to her core. Insinuating his hand between her legs, he traced taunting little circles over the thin covering of silk.

"You've got too many clothes on," he murmured, slipping one finger under the lacy edge of elastic. In one smooth movement, the scrap of fabric was drawn down her legs and tossed to the floor. When his fingers sought to return to their maddening play, she caught his hand.

Every cell in her body was screaming for him. Unable to voice the need escalating so rapidly within her, she could only say with her hands and the insistence in her kiss how badly she needed for him to assuage the desire he'd created.

Adam felt that need as forcefully as he did his own. He was promising her nothing, yet he was offering her everything he was capable of giving. He could taste her longing, feel it in the warmth of her supple body as she curved her legs around his. He'd wanted to explore every inch of her, to discover all there was to know about every seductive curve and crevice. But the demanding ache in his loins wouldn't allow that now.

Urging her thighs apart with his knee, he held back long enough for her to accept his weight and eased himself forward. Just before he gave himself up to the exquisite heat enveloping him, he saw the woman beneath him close her eyes in complete surrender. His woman. Stephanie.

Adam. Over and over she whispered his name, glorying in the beauty of the world they were creating. It was theirs, an Olympus no other mortal could ever climb. The gentle words of encouragement he offered, sweet endearments to meld with the sweeter sensations engulfing them, begged her to join him at its apex. She allowed him to lead her, to be her Apollo and carry her on his golden chariot through the constellations bearing the names of the ancient gods. And when they burst upon that bright, sunlit place, she knew her heart had found its home.

Adam had found something, too. The heavy thud of his heart had quieted while he held her close, each even beat magnifying that unfamiliar sense of peace. But now, in the lengthening quiet, it was being replaced with a feeling that wasn't quite so comfortable.

"Stephanie." The sound of her name clung like honey to his lips as he breathed in the clean, flowery scent of her hair. Lifting his weight to his elbows, he stroked back the ginger-colored tendrils laying against her cheek. "You okay?"

The faintest trace of a smile touched her mouth. "I'm wonderful."

"True. But are you all right?"

The concern in his voice must have made her ignore the way he'd deliberately misinterpreted her response. Her eyes opened, the heavy fringe of her lashes fluttering as she blinked up at him. "Why wouldn't I be?"

"I don't know," he evaded, feeling her hands ease down his back when he lifted his shoulders in a shrug. "I mean, I do know, but..." It wasn't like him to be so inarticulate. Realizing that he'd never before wanted the assurance he was seeking, he covered his anxiety by kissing the smooth skin of her forehead.

Her legs were curved around his. Now he felt their smoothness as she shifted beneath him to ease them away. "Adam," she began, apprehension straining her voice. "What's wrong?"

It was his own insecurity that was causing her to withdraw from his embrace. He'd never felt insecure about anything, and he didn't like the feeling any better than he liked the way she was trying to move away from him. If he said what was on his mind, he could alleviate, or compound, both problems.

"Stay here," he said with more confidence than he felt, and pushed down with his hips to keep her where she was. He probably shouldn't have done that. His motion, coupled with the way her abdominal muscles tightened, triggered the same desire she had so thoroughly sated only minutes ago. Willing himself not to move, he finally found the words he needed to say. "The only thing wrong is that I'm afraid you might...you might wish this hadn't happened...and stop moving like that unless you want it to happen again."

She laid perfectly still. For about three seconds. Then, doing a fairly commendable job of hiding what looked very much like relief, she took his face between her hands. "I won't ever regret it," she assured him in a low, seductive whisper. "Can I move now?"

"I think that will depend on what you mean. If you want to move away from me, then the answer's no."

"What if I mean, like this?"

The moan that attached itself to his sharp intake of breath seemed to indicate that her motion met with his approval. So did the yearning she felt in his kiss and the sweet seduction of his hands roaming down her sides.

How could she ever regret what she was sharing with him? It was too late to allow uncertainties to intrude anyway. Having finally given in to that nagging sense of the inevitable, she'd acknowledged the truth compelling her now. The fates had decreed it—and she was in love with him. The magic had been there since the moment they met.

"What the—?" Adam rolled over to find himself face-to-face, or more aptly, nose to nose, with something warm and furry.

"That's his pillow." Propping herself up on her elbow, Stephanie yawned and blinked into the darkness. "No wonder you're always stuffy in the morning. How'd he get in here? I thought he was in his playpen."

"He was, but I brought him in so his whining wouldn't wake you up."

In the shadows, she saw Adam run his fingers through his rumpled hair. "I didn't mean to fall asleep. What time is it? Real time," he clarified, "not whatever it says on your clock."

As quickly as her sleep-fogged brain would allow, she subtracted twenty minutes from the indicated Roman numerals glowing from her nightstand. "Two-fifteen."

Adam rolled over again, turning his back to the surprisingly quiet puppy to gather Stephanie in his arms. A long, lingering kiss was pressed to her lips. "Tell me I don't have to go home."

"You don't have to go home, Adam."

"Thank you," he whispered, guiding her head to his shoulder.

He always woke up in his own bed. For some reason he preferred to avoid the implication of spending the entire night with a woman. Yet, here he was, not even questioning why he had no intention of leaving. The only thing he was wondering about was why he was also sleeping with her dog.

Every three minutes for the past hour, Stephanie had glanced from the grout she was working between the tiles behind her sink to the clock on the stove. Adam had said he'd be a little late getting here this afternoon, but she'd expected him long before now. What if he didn't want to see her? What if he was having the regrets he'd said he didn't want her to have? What had he meant by that anyway? What if...?

Turning with a start when she heard the sharp knock at the back door, she tried not to look disappointed when it swung open.

"That must have been some tennis date." Linda offered her observation from where she was leaning with her arms crossed against the doorjamb.

Stephanie knew exactly what had prompted that remark. When Adam had rushed out of the house at seven o'clock this morning, Linda's husband was pulling out of their driveway. Linda always sent Ed off with a wave from their front window.

Zeus's mad dash across the floor offered a temporary reprieve from comment. "Grab him, will you? If I pick him up, I'll have to give him a bath."

"I can see that." Linda's eyes flew from the beige, puttylike stuff sticking to Stephanie's fingers to the puppy charging toward her. Rather than picking him up, though, she just closed the door and watched all four of Zeus's legs stiffen as he slid to a swerving halt. Now that he wasn't moving with the velocity of a rocket, she bent over to scoop him up. "Foiled again. Huh, sport?"

"Do you think Matthew and Micky would like to take him for a walk again today? He could really use the exercise. Being cooped up in..."

"You know they would," Linda interrupted with a wry smile. "Stop trying to change the subject."

"What subject?" Turning to avoid the knowing eyes of her friend, she dabbed on the last fingerful of grout and reached for her sponge. "This stuff is so messy."

"If you think replacing a half-dozen tiles is a mess, you should try doing a whole bathroom. And you know darn good and well what I'm talking about. Adam spent the night, didn't he?"

"You know he did." The nagging, uncomfortable thought she'd been trying to bury finally surfaced. Keeping her back to Linda while she wiped up the tiles, Stephanie muttered, "By now so does half the neighborhood."

"I doubt that. Mrs. Dobbs is a late sleeper. The first thing I noticed right after I saw Adam jump into his car was that her drapes were still closed. Where is he anyway? There's usually a mob in your backyard this time of day."

"He won't be bringing his students anymore."

"Why not?"

Relieved to have the topic temporarily diverted, she began to tell Linda about the discovery Adam had made yesterday. She was very careful to give Adam's explanation, or lack of one, as to why Dino couldn't be a unicorn, but she also couldn't help allowing her own open-minded opinion to intrude. After all, stranger things had happened, and a person couldn't rule out a possibility just because something was unfamiliar.

As she spoke, she was barely aware that, for once, Linda was remaining perfectly silent. She also didn't realize that she was beginning to digress when she stood back to inspect the job she'd just finished. "You know," she said, looping the towel through the door handle of the refrigerator after she'd dried her hands, "I think that just might explain why it can't work."

Normally, Linda had no difficulty picking up on Stephanie's enigmatic comments. She apparently did now. "Explain why what can't work?"

"Me and Adam."

"You just lost me."

"Come on into the bedroom while I change, and I'll explain it to you. It's really very simple," she continued while Linda followed her down the hall. "Adam won't believe it's a unicorn until he proves it is, and I'll believe it is until he proves it isn't."

Linda perched herself on the edge of the neatly made bed while Stephanie rummaged through her closet. She'd been so obviously enthralled with Dino's tentative identification that it took her a moment to untangle Stephanie's logic. "I get it . . . I think."

"All I'm saying is that there's really nothing we agree on. We don't even like to read the same stuff. There wasn't a single novel on his bookshelves. All he had were things on photography and old ruins and—"

"When did you see his bookshelves?" Linda cut in.

"We stopped by his apartment the other day so he could change clothes after we played tennis. I was only in his living room, and only for about two minutes, but it was enough to tell me we'd never find a compromise in the interior-design department. Beside the fact that his persimmon walls nearly scream at you, he's into black leather and . . ."

"Sounds kinky."

"Will you be serious?"

"I will, if you will. Listen to yourself. Everything you've mentioned is so trivial."

"Taken individually, I agree with you. Those were just examples, anyway." Her work clothes were tossed in the hamper, and a pink raglan-sleeved blouse was being pulled over her head. "Add all the little things up, toss in the bigger ones and you have two very incompatible people. A relationship can hardly be built on differing opinions."

Their most recent difference of opinion had occurred just this morning. Even while he was kissing her breathless at the front door, Adam was insisting that it was silly to allow Zeus to sleep so close to her. She'd refrained from comment, but only because she'd started sneezing.

Linda handed Stephanie the pink shorts she'd laid on the bed. "I'd say you're doing pretty well for two people who don't have a whole lot in common. Don't worry about it, and just wait and see what develops."

Sighing as she tucked her blouse into her shorts, Stephanie tossed a cryptic glance at the smiling redhead. "Something already has."

"That was obvious enough when I saw his car this morning." Giving a little bounce on the mattress, Linda grinned.

If Stephanie had been in the habit of blushing, she probably would have now. Not only was Linda outspoken, but there were also times when she could be quite outrageous. "That's not what I'm talking about."

"Well, what then?"

"I love him."

"I knew that."

"You did?"

"Sure. You won't go out to lunch after class, because you're always in such a hurry to get back here. I've asked you to go shopping three times, but you've always had some excuse not to go until after he's gone and then it's too late for me to go. You can't say his name without your voice getting softer. And the way you keep watching the clock tells me he was supposed to be here and because he isn't you're getting nervous. Shall I go on?''

"You don't understand," Stephanie replied, ignoring the question. "I'm in love with him, but he can never be in love with me."

"Nonsense."

"Linda, Adam doesn't believe in love."

"He told you that?"

"Not in so many words, but I definitely got the picture."

Linda's smile crumpled. "Then he probably doesn't believe in marriage, fidelity, hearth, home and family, either."

"I think that's a safe conclusion to draw." Still not sure how she could feel so wonderfully happy and so incredibly miserable at the same time, Stephanie willed herself to simply accept the facts. She loved Adam. Adam didn't love her. But he did care. All she could do was make the best of what she had to work with, and that meant dwelling only on the positive aspects of the situation. "I wish he'd call or something." That wasn't quite the aspect she wanted to dwell on.

"You never did say where he was."

"That's because I don't know. He had a class to teach this morning, but he didn't say what his plans were…other than he'd be late getting here. Since he used to show up at noon, I assumed he meant midafternoon. But it's after five now."

Her ability to overlook the negative must have taken a hike. By the time she and Linda returned to the kitchen and settled themselves at the table with cans of diet cola, Stephanie was pouring out all the "what ifs" she'd been listing just before Linda arrived. The more she said, the more convinced she became that Adam had either decided that last night was a mistake, or he'd gotten in a car wreck in his rush to be on time for his class this morning.

"I'm sure he's got a reasonable explanation," Linda offered, "so stop worrying about it. Being in love sometimes has a tendency to make a person's imagination a little overactive. You're just going through the normal set of insecurities, that's all." Strolling over to the utility room, she dropped her empty can into Stephanie's recycling sack. "Now that I've offered that sage bit of wisdom, I think I'd better get home and get dinner over with so I can hit the books." Her nose wrinkled at that thought. "The next time you want to take a class, make it one without homework, would you? What was it we were supposed to read for tomorrow, anyway?"

"The chapter on Bellerophon. He's the one who rode Pegasus."

"Oh, yes. The great winged horse." Linda tipped her head toward the backyard, her eyes twinkling. "Think we'll get to unicorns?"

Neither the smile that had started to form nor Stephanie's reply got any farther than the edge of her mouth. The familiar roar of a bright red Porsche had just screeched to silence in front of her house.

"Take a deep breath," Linda coached, "and try not to look so relieved."

"I don't think it's relief I'm feeling at the moment."

"Well, try not to look so nervous then. Act a little aloof. That ought to make him sweat."

"Why would I want to do that?"

"Because of what he put you through. You just spent the past thirty minutes wondering if he was dying, or worse, if he'd dumped you and..."

The peal of the doorbell brought an abrupt end to Linda's recount—and brought Stephanie unsteadily to her feet. Other than the first time he'd come here and this morning's exit, he'd never used the front door. He always came around back. Was that an omen?

Zeus had already deposited himself in the entryway. Linda walked over and deposited him in the playpen. She knew the routine.

Taking it upon herself to open the door since Stephanie was only staring at it, Linda glared up at Adam's somewhat surprised expression. "You could have called," she stated bluntly. Ignoring both the blank look on his face and the large object he was carrying, she marched down the steps.

Adam stepped inside, his head still turned to the open door. "What was that all about?"

Her eyes on the long, three-sided basket dangling from his right hand, Stephanie walked toward him. Each step brought a silent reminder that she was to act aloof. He didn't have to know... "I was worried about you," she said in a soft voice. She never had been a very good actress.

His head swiveled around, his gaze sweeping over her. There was at once incomprehension and warmth tingeing the cool blue of his eyes. "Why?"

Half of her fears were very carefully kept to herself. All he was allowed to hear was the other half. "Because I was afraid something might have happened to you. When you said you'd be a little late, I...well...you're usually so punctual and I thought that by a 'little' you only meant an hour or two, so..." The more she said, the deeper she dug herself, so she decided that she should just shut her mouth.

"So you started to worry," he completed, pushing the door closed with his foot. Two strides brought him squarely in front of her. "I've never had anyone worry about me before. I think I like it."

That was about the last thing she'd expected him to say, and it did a very effective job of calming her insecurities. So did the very thorough kiss he worked over her mouth when he tipped her chin up with his finger.

Smiling down at her, he dropped his hand. "I brought you something. I would have been here sooner, but I had to go to three different places to find the right size. Think it's too big?"

The doggy bed he was holding out was large enough for three puppies the size of Zeus. "It's perfect," she said, hoping she didn't sound too puzzled.

"Good. I don't think it's healthy for someone with an allergy to dogs to be sleeping with one. You can put his pillow in here, and he can sleep beside your bed."

Most men would have shown up with flowers. Adam showed up with a doggy bed. Eternally practical, and thoughtful enough to be concerned about her health. That had to mean something. Didn't it?

Neither one of them had mentioned his name, but Zeus knew they were talking about him. His tail was moving like a whip. Lowering herself beside the playpen, she scratched his head with one hand and held up the basket with the other. "Look at what Adam brought you, punkin. Your very own bed. How's that?"

"I didn't buy it for him. I bought it for you."

"Oh, I couldn't possibly fit in there. It's too small."

The teasing in her eyes met the dull look he was giving her. "You know that's not what I meant."

She knew. She also knew that it was ridiculous for a grown man to act the way Adam did toward Zeus. He pretty much ignored the puppy unless she was holding him, and then he'd scowl at the way Zeus would curl up on her chest. And whenever Adam got closer than a few feet away, Zeus would start to growl. The two of them actually acted like they were jealous of each other. She could understand an animal developing that kind of an attachment to its mistress, but would Adam...

Not pleased with the connotation in her uncompleted thought, she started to dismiss it. The effort was unnecessary. The strain in Adam's voice accomplished the feat for her.

"I think we need to talk, Stephanie."

Seven

With a theatrical flare, Professor Markham Mitchell closed the textbook on the podium, and peered over the top of his wire-rimmed half glasses. "In conclusion, one must admit that, while a mortal's imagination is capable of conjuring fantastic images, the similarities in the depiction of Pegasus by persons who had no contact with one another are too incredible to be dismissed as coincidence. We will explore this conclusion further in our study of the goat god, Pan, when we meet next Tuesday."

Giving his neatly trimmed Vandyke beard one last stroke, he took off his glasses and, folding them, placed them in his jacket pocket. That meant class was dismissed, but Stephanie missed the predictable signal—not surprising since she'd also missed ninety percent of what he'd said.

The noise level in the room increased perceptibly. Books slammed, and the scrape of desk seats against the floor joined the shuffle of feet. With a guilty start, Stephanie blinked up at the empty lecturn. Having just spent the past hour and a half with her body in one place and her mind in another, it took a moment for the two to get back together. Was class over? Already?

The number of students pouring out the door seemed to indicate that it was. So did the murmur of voices now filling the room.

"Listening to that guy almost makes me believe this stuff," a young man with a neck like a tree stump muttered as he passed her desk.

"You were actually listening?" the studious-looking blonde behind him taunted. "I could have sworn all you jocks ever did in class was catch up on your sleep."

Stephanie slumped a little lower in her chair. She was wondering if anyone had noticed how little attention *she'd* paid to the class when Linda leaned across the aisle separating them. Her voice was a conspiratorial whisper. "I think she likes him. She's actually wearing mascara today."

Linda pulled back to allow a few more of their classmates to pass. Her grin widened when she saw Stephanie look up at the couple and smile in agreement. Picking up her book, she slid from her seat. "I'm going to go ask Professor Mitchell for next week's assignments. The last thing I want is to get back from vacation and have to cram for a test or something. You want to wait for me here, or outside?"

"Outside," Stephanie returned, and closed the cover on the blank page in her notebook. Well, not quite blank. There was a very ornately scrawled *Adam* in the upper right-hand corner. She'd traced over it at least a dozen times—which was about the same number of times she'd repeated the lecture she'd given herself after Adam had left last night. It was the same one she'd been going over just now.

Sighing, she jammed her notebook into her tote bag and joined the crush of people moving out into the hall. It was easy enough to tell herself that she had to curb this propensity to panic she'd so suddenly developed. It was putting that instruction into effect that was going to need work.

When Adam had so bluntly announced that they needed to talk, Stephanie had immediately experienced a reaction that, until yesterday, was totally foreign to her nature. She had suspected the worst.

Prepared to hear that he viewed what had happened the night before as a mistake, it had taken several agonizing seconds for her to realize that the subject he'd started talking about while he paced in front of her sofa *wasn't* their relationship. It was this latest development with Dino. Adam had explained that, since he'd now be working alone, there was no way he could meet his original deadline—and that would mean another delay for her pool contractor.

If she hadn't been so busy trying not to look like she'd just been handed a reprieve, she could have strangled him for scaring her like that.

Adam didn't know that he'd caused her to age fifty years during those past few minutes. All Stephanie had let him see was her calm acceptance of the delay, and maybe a hint of disappointment when he'd announced that he couldn't stay because he had to meet Dave. Two minutes later, while he was kissing her goodbye, she'd had the feeling he was still trying to figure out why something that had been so important just a few weeks ago—the completion of her pool—now didn't seem to matter at all.

What mattered to Stephanie now, as she checked her watch for the third time, was that she was going to be late. According to Adam's revised schedule, he wouldn't be arriving at her house for over an hour, but she was beginning to wonder if she'd get there before he did. Why was it taking so long for Linda to get her assignments?

Stephanie had been waiting beside Linda's locked car for almost twenty minutes. Wondering if a rescue might be in order, she pulled her tote bag off the hood and slung it over her shoulder. Professor Mitchell had a tendency to turn a two-minute conversation into a lecture, given an audience and an opportunity. It could very well be that Linda was that audience.

Or, had been. Just as Stephanie rounded the front of the car, she saw a head of light copper curls bouncing along the far side of the hedges lining the parking lot. A few seconds later, Linda was rushing toward her.

"Oh, Stephanie. I'm sorry. I had no idea that was going to take so long. There were a couple of kids ahead of me and then the professor had to find his assignment sheets, and when I told him about Dino, he forgot all about the assignments, and I was halfway out the door before I remembered why I'd even gone up to talk to him and then he finally found..."

Stephanie grabbed Linda's arm as she hurried past to unlock the passenger door, bringing her and her rapid-fire explanation to a jolting stop. "You told him about Dino?"

For a moment Linda's expression was totally blank. Then, her hand flew to her open mouth. "Oh, God. Did you ask me not to say anything about what you told me?"

Not at all certain why she'd just felt something sink in her stomach, Stephanie shook her head. "No. I didn't. It's just..." A dismissing smile preceded her muttered, "Never mind. Just one of my dumb premonitions. Let's get you home so you can start packing."

"I've got to do laundry before I can do that. You sure I didn't say something I shouldn't have."

"I'm sure," Stephanie said, wishing that she really could be.

"That's a relief. Want to stop for a banana split?"

"You don't have time for that. You've got a family to get ready to go to the mountains tomorrow, remember? And I've got to get home before..."

"Before Adam gets there," Linda drawled. "You're not any fun anymore, Stephanie. I can't remember the last time you turned down a banana split."

Neither could Stephanie. But then she was also having trouble remembering the last time she'd been late for anything. Incredible as it seemed, she hadn't kept Linda waiting for her this morning, nor last Thursday, either. She'd even been early for her dental appointment Monday.

It was Adam who was late—by a good two hours.

Stephanie had steadfastly refused to indulge in the panic she'd subjected herself to yesterday. By the time his Porsche screeched into her driveway, she'd called three girlfriends she hadn't talked to since school let out, made a luncheon date with one of them, then called her dad to order the wallpaper she'd finally selected—all in an attempt to avoid wondering what was keeping Adam.

After all, it could have been any of a number of things. A student. Car trouble. One of the women he knew.

Giving Zeus a conciliatory pat when she put him in his playpen, she had to admit that her attempts at diversion weren't always successful.

"Hi," she greeted easily when she opened the back door. "How'd things go at the tar pits?" Thinking she'd carried out her composed act rather well, and that what she'd just said was a rather innovative twist to the more conventional, "How'd things go at the office?" her smile widened.

Adam wasn't smiling at all.

Uh-oh, she thought when he stepped past her without saying a word. Either the new location for his biweekly labs wasn't working out, or he'd decided they...

Clamping a mental hand over that overactive mental mouth, she closed the door and walked over to where he'd leaned against the counter. His arms were crossed over a brilliant blue polo shirt, his long denim-clad legs were crossed at the ankles and his expression was just plain cross.

His tone wasn't particularly pleasant, either. "Do you know where I've been for the past two hours?"

The arches of her eyebrows snapped up. "At the tar pits?" she ventured.

"Try again."

"Dave's?"

A muscle in his jaw jumped as he shook his head. "Keep going."

"Are we playing twenty questions or something? How could I possibly know where you've been?"

"Because of your friend's big mouth."

"What fr—?"

It wasn't necessary for her to complete the question, let alone the word. He was talking about Linda, and the reason for the odd premonition she'd felt earlier came into startling focus. Something had happened. That was obvious enough. It was only the magnitude of the problem she was concerned with at the moment. If the knot in her stomach was an accurate gauge, it was definitely a big one.

Adam wasn't quite furious, but he was close enough. The tight rein he had on his temper was evident in every clipped word. "I stopped by my office to drop off some papers after I left La Brea, Stephanie. When I got there, I found that professor of yours waiting for me. The man hadn't even introduced himself before he started demanding that I share my 'discovery' with him and telling me that as a gentleman and a scholar I was severely derelict in my responsibilities to the academic community by withholding information of 'such monumental significance.'"

As Stephanie's eyes widened, she bit down on her lower lip. It was no wonder Adam was so angry. For Professor Mitchell to have attacked his character like that was not only infuriating but it was also inexcusable. The man didn't even know Adam.

But Stephanie did. He had more integrity than anyone she'd ever met. The last thing he'd ever do was shirk his responsibilities. She was about to tell him that, and add a few other ego-salving compliments, when his glare hardened.

"Whatever," he began in a tone just this side of daunting, "possessed you to tell Linda that Dino was a unicorn?"

A moment ago Stephanie had felt a surge of protective anger. Now, all she felt was defensive. "I didn't tell her it was a unicorn. In fact I made a point of telling her that you didn't know what it was yet. What I said was that *I* thought it..."

"Dammit, Stephanie. Why did you mention it to her at all?"

"Because I tell Linda everything! Don't you have someone you talk to about all the things going on in your life?"

Of all the people he knew, the only one he ever spoke of with any regularity was Dave, but that was only in a professional context. It wasn't particularly surprising then, when he confirmed the conclusion she'd already drawn—that Adam kept his private life to himself.

"I've never found it necessary to discuss everything that happens to me with someone else. If you need a confidante, you should pick one that will keep her..." Apparently aware that attacking Stephanie's best friend was not the wisest thing to do, he cut himself off.

He hadn't caught himself quickly enough, though. Seething, Stephanie lifted her chin in a regal tilt. "I never asked her not to say anything about it, so you can hardly accuse her of breaking a confidence."

"The point is that she said something she had no business knowing in the first place."

"She didn't know that!"

"You did."

"I did not!"

Adam's voice, though decidedly tight, was still at a normal level, which made her realize that hers had increased by a couple of decibels. Immediately she lowered her tone. All it did was make what she said next sound like an excuse, and that wasn't how she'd meant it to sound at all. "You never said I couldn't talk about it."

Now that she'd toned down, he'd grown louder. "I didn't think it would be necessary. I know you want to believe there's something to all that mythology business, but I also thought you'd realize just how improbable it would be to find proof of something like that in your own backyard. For God's sake, Stephanie, common sense should have told you that much. Just like common sense should have told you what could happen if something like this gets out.''

With that, he abruptly turned. Slapping both hands flat on the counter, he lowered his head and drew a deep breath. He was clearly trying to regain the control he'd just lost. From the tension visible in the rigid cords of his broad shoulders, that feat was taking a considerable effort.

A fair amount of effort was being exercised a few feet away, too. It was taking everything she had to keep from telling him she was sorry. She wasn't going to tell him that his crack about her lacking common sense was probably right, either. If she had any sense at all, she'd never have fallen in love with him.

"I'm not going to apologize for what I believe, Adam."

Silence hung heavy for several seconds. Refusing to say another word before he acknowledged what she'd just said, she hugged her arms over the knot in her stomach.

When he turned to face her, there was a glint of admiration relieving the irritation still in his eyes. "I'm not asking you to. What I am asking is that you keep your mouth shut about all this unicorn stuff. Okay?''

She didn't like the way he'd phrased that, but she wasn't going to push it now that he'd gotten himself calmed down. When he was upset, he was a little frightening. "Okay. What about Professor Mitchell, though? What did you tell him?''

"What I've been telling you all along."

"I can't believe he settled for that."

"He didn't. The only way I could get the guy off my back was to promise that he'd be the first to know what it is as soon as I figure it out. After spending an hour talking until I was blue in the face, he finally agreed that a definite conclusion might be premature at this point." Combing his fingers through his hair, he let out a slow breath and started back across the kitchen. "I better get to work."

The preoccupied look Adam wore so often was firmly in place when he walked out the door. About fifteen seconds later, he was back.

"I forgot something," he announced.

In one swift movement he'd caught her by the waist, and his mouth was moving firmly over hers. His tongue darted inward at her gasp, tangling with her own, then began an intimate foray that left her completely dazed.

Leaving his palms against the sides of her breasts as he set her back from him, Adam gave her a slightly crooked smile. "Thought I'd better say hello. Do you have plans tonight?"

The man had a definite knack of throwing curves. One minute, he'd looked like it would have given him great pleasure to throttle her. The next, he was kissing her socks off. Feeling decidedly off balance, she whispered no.

"Good. Let's go out to dinner."

"I thought you were mad at me."

"I tried to be." His head lowered, but he seemed to change his mind about where he was aiming and dropped his kiss on the tip of her nose instead of her mouth. "Let me work out back until six or so. You be ready, and we'll run by my place so I can change before we go out. Make reservations anywhere you want."

"You're giving me carte blanche? Don't you know that could be expensive?"

"Not as expensive as having you burn down your house with that barbecue of yours."

He was obviously alluding to the amount of fuel she'd used to fix Zeus his treat the morning she'd put him in the utility room. "You need a decent flame to get a good hamburger," she defended.

"I like my meat rare, Stephanie."

"That figures."

"What?"

"Never mind. I'll be ready at six."

She was ready at five-thirty. An all-time record made even more impressive because she'd had a devil of a time deciding what to wear. The pink linen was too "sweet." Her mint silk with its nonexistent back, too sexy. A whole closet later, she'd settled for a deceptively simple, white sleeveless jersey that did marvelous things for her figure. It also made her feel deliciously feminine. The soft fabric brushed her skin as gently as Adam's fingers had caressed the unrestrained fullness of her breasts when...

The quick shake of her head was followed by a long, slowly expelled breath. Wondering if she'd used too much blush or if it was the bold path her thoughts kept taking that gave her cheeks so much color, she leaned toward her dresser mirror. The woman smiling back at her with a slightly wicked gleam in her eyes winked.

Must be the thoughts, Stephanie concluded, contemplating whether or not she'd really just winked at herself. The peach-tinted blush was fine.

A heady sort of anticipation had accompanied the course of her mental wanderings. Last night, Adam had left after a few too-brief kisses because of his appoint-

ment with Dave. The same raw urgency she'd felt in him
then had been evident when he'd held her just a short
while ago—though he'd once again curbed it because he
had work to do. The restraint he'd exercised had been
quite noticeable.

There would be none of those distractions tonight.
They could talk, and argue, and enjoy their companion-
able silences knowing the evening was theirs. Every minute they spent together seemed to strengthen the bond
growing between them. Each touch increased the need to
physically reinforce that commitment. For her, anyway.
She could only guess at how Adam interpreted his feelings.

Having finally met the man she'd been waiting for all
her life, Stephanie wasn't going to let a little thing like his
refusal to admit the existence of an emotion keep her
from loving him. She'd simply accept whatever part of
himself he was willing to share and guard it as the most
precious of gifts.

A soft smile touched her lips. "He said he tried to stay
upset with me," she told Zeus, who was curled up beside
her bed chewing on her slipper. "If he couldn't, that must
mean something. Huh, punkin?"

If it did, Stephanie wasn't at all sure what it was. By the
time she and Adam had ordered their predinner drinks at
the quietly sedate Continental restaurant, she was more
than a little confused by the mixed signals he'd been
sending her.

When Adam had come in to wash up before they left,
he'd practically stripped her dress right off her with his
searing gaze. Then he'd gruffly announced that they were
going to be late, not saying another word until they were
separated by the console in his sports car. "You look

beautiful," he'd said, leaning over to capture her face between his hands.

After thoroughly kissing her, he'd held her hand all the way to his apartment, but hadn't come anywhere near her once they were inside. She'd waited in his living room, skeptically eyeing the polished skull of some small animal sitting on a lacquered table, while Adam had showered and changed. Then, she'd barely had time to notice how magnificent he looked in his tan slacks and rich brown sports coat before he'd hustled her out the door. Now, sitting across from him in the crowded restaurant, she was once again being visually disrobed.

I wish she'd worn a bra, Adam sighed to himself and took another sip of his Scotch. The top of her dress was loose fitting, one of those blousy things that draped down to a belt and a straight skirt. Quite modest really. But the stuff it was made out of clung in the more strategic places—like her hips—and gave a suggestion of the high little breasts he couldn't seem to move his eyes from. He couldn't help but wonder if the air-conditioning was making her chilly.

"Would you..." Setting his drink down, he cleared his throat and tried again. "Would you like my jacket?"

The question must have sounded a little odd to her. "Your jacket?"

"I thought it might be a little cool in here for you."

She didn't know it, but as she pushed her glass of wine forward and crossed her arms on the table, the ulterior motive behind his gesture had just been accomplished. From the ease of her smile, it was apparent she mistook his offer for thoughtfulness. "I'm quite comfortable. But thanks."

Now that he wasn't quite so distracted, he could feel himself starting to relax a little. Or maybe it was the gentleness, the kind of quiet serenity in her smile that was relieving some of his inner tension. In another hour or so, he'd be alone with her again. For now, he wouldn't think about that, though. He'd just let himself enjoy being with her, then clamp a lid on his libido when he took her home.

As he sat there watching her smile at the waiter who'd just handed her a menu, he knew it would only make matters worse if he made love with her again. She was clearly not the type of woman who engaged in casual sex, and the more intimate they became, the greater the chances of her being hurt when it came time for them to part. That had to happen eventually. It always did. He was quite content with his life just the way it was—or the way it had been before he met Stephanie. Since he'd known her, things hadn't seemed quite so...predictable.

The last thought reminded him of the very unpredictable reaction he'd experienced a couple of hours ago—and the message he'd forgotten to give Stephanie. "Your father called while you were in the shower," he said conversationally, and marveled again at the stab of jealousy he'd felt when he'd first heard the male voice on the other end of the line.

Since Stephanie had kept her parents apprised of the goings-on in her backyard, it was safe to assume that her father hadn't thought anything untoward about Adam's having answered her phone. "Did he say he'd call back?"

"No. He just said to tell you your wallpaper will be in Saturday and, if you want to come pick it up, plan on spending the weekend. Your sister will be there."

Though Stephanie would have loved to see her family, she didn't want to spend the weekend in San Diego. Knowing it was a long shot, since Adam's schedule indicated he'd be working on Dino, she gave in to impulse and asked anyway. "I think I'll just make it a quick trip on Sunday. Would you like to drive down with me?"

She already knew what his answer would be. If something wasn't on his schedule, it simply didn't happen.

"Sure," he replied, surprising them both. Snapping his menu open, he quickly added, "I don't trust that car of yours, so I'll drive you. They've got great steaks here. Want one?"

There was an old expression, something about not looking a gift horse in the mouth, that reminded Stephanie not to question his unexpected agreement. She also wasn't going to dwell on the usual implications of taking a man home to meet the family. Adam was just being...well, practical. "I think I'll try the Veal Oscar."

"Why do you want to ruin a good piece of meat with all that sauce and stuff?"

"Probably for the same reason you like your steak so rare it jumps onto your fork for you."

His eyes narrowed, but not enough to hide the teasing smile lighting their cool blue depths. "We do have our differences, don't we?"

Picking up her wine, she gave him a wry smile. "I was wondering if you'd noticed."

"Oh, I have, Stephanie. Believe me, I have."

Two hours later, all Stephanie was noticing was Adam's gradual withdrawal as they neared her house. His teasing had stopped somewhere between the restaurant and the parking lot. Conversation had come to a halt about six blocks ago. Now, with only the brief flashes of streetlamps revealing the stoic set to his mouth, he took his hand from where it had been resting on top of hers on his thigh and curled it over the knob on the gearshift.

Stephanie slowly pulled her hand to her lap and threaded her fingers together. It was too soon for him to switch gears, so she could only interpret what he'd done as another step in his inexplicable transition.

Maybe it wasn't so inexplicable. It was always possible that, even though he'd denied it earlier, he was still upset at her over what had happened with Professor Mitchell. She was about to ask him that when she saw his hand jerk down on the shift and he tersely muttered, "To hell with it."

Seconds later he'd pulled the car to a jolting stop by the curb and was leaning across the console. "Come here," he commanded, taking her by the shoulders. "There's no way I'll be able to kiss you the way I want on your front porch, so I might as well do it now."

Not at all certain what had prompted his puzzling statement—and not about to waste any time thinking about it now that he was finally giving her the kiss she'd been aching for all night—she curved her arms around his neck. Gladly accepting the hungry demands of his tongue, she leaned forward, trying to make the contact the console wouldn't allow. Adam's moan of frustration at that barrier met her own.

Pushing his seat back, he lifted her across the console and onto his lap. With his arm around her and his free hand resting on her hip, he continued the kiss he'd barely broken.

It didn't matter that something metallic was poking the back of her knee or that one of her strappy heels was now dangling from her foot. Stephanie felt herself melting against him, relishing the solid warmth enfolding her. Whenever he held her, the doubts constantly clouding her mind vanished. His simplest touch could make their differences seem almost inconsequential. If only she could have that kind of power over him.

It hardly seemed fair that Cupid should have flung his arrows so carelessly—that her heart had been pierced with the gold-tipped arrow of love while Adam had intercepted the leaden one of indifference. Indifference only to love, though, not to passion.

Cupid, Eros to the Greeks, had been born of the god Chaos. And chaos was what Adam was wreaking on her senses now. She could feel his hardness pressing her hip. When he filled his palm with her breast, she shifted against him with a low moan. Increasing the pressure of his hand, his tongue captured the audible sign of her arousal.

Long moments later, the rasp of his voice broke the sensual oblivion surrounding them.

"What am I doing?" His tight whisper fanned her heated cheek. "I only wanted to kiss you."

"That's all you are doing," she whispered back, slipping her fingers through his hair to draw his head down again.

Instead of allowing her to deepen the kiss, he moved his lips to her cheek. Rather than let her hand slip over the solid breadth of his chest, he caught it with his, holding it firmly against her hip. "Don't!"

Stunned by his fierce whisper, she stiffened.

"Oh, honey," he said, sighing. "I'm sorry." Pressing her head to his shoulder, he held her so tightly she could barely breathe. "I didn't mean that the way it sounded. It's just that if we don't stop this, I'll probably wind up saying to hell with the only attempt at chivalry I've ever made and take you right here in the front seat." His grip on her eased. A moment later, his arms had fallen away. "I'd better get you home."

Untangling herself as best she could, she slid back to her own side. The self-deprecation she'd heard in his voice had confused her as much as what he'd just said. Chivalry? What was he talking about?

In stunned silence she sat there staring at the way he was gripping the steering wheel. She wished it wasn't so dark. The car was parked under a tree, the nearest streetlamp at the other end of the block. Adam's face was nothing but a shadow. She could only guess at what his expression might be.

When several seconds had passed and he'd made no move to put the car in gear, she could bear her confusion no longer.

"What's wrong, Adam?"

"Nothing."

"I don't believe you."

"I didn't think you would."

"Then will you please tell me what happened just now?"

To her surprise he didn't try to evade the question. "I remembered that I can't make love to you."

"Can't?"

"Won't."

"Why?" she swallowed.

"Just leave it, okay?"

She wished she could, but the ache growing inside her needed to know why it was there. "Does this have something to do with . . . with one of your girlfriends?" She'd started to say Diane or Barbara or Cindy. Somehow it had seemed easier to conclude with the more ambiguous term. She didn't want to know the woman's identity. "I mean, if you're involved with . . ."

"Hell no," he muttered, apparently realizing the track her thoughts had taken. "You're the only woman I've been 'involved with' in weeks. For God's sake, Stephanie, do you honestly think I'd do something like that to you?''

If by 'something like that' he meant sleeping with her while he was sleeping with someone else, she really didn't think so. Even if she'd allowed herself to think about it, the common sense he'd said she lacked would have told her he had no time for anyone else.

Adam didn't know it, but he'd just told her something very important in the way he'd asked that question. She mattered to him. A lot.

"I suppose not," she said quietly when she felt him growing impatient at her silence.

"Well, you suppose right. This whole situation is confusing enough without dragging an issue like that into it. The one thing I'm trying not to do is hurt you."

An awkward silence filled the interior of the small car. Blessing the darkness she'd cursed only a moment ago, Stephanie kept her eyes straight ahead. For a few uncomfortable seconds, she could feel Adam staring at her profile before putting the car in gear and pulling back out onto the street.

As if he'd just read her thoughts, he muttered, "I don't understand this any better than you do."

It was the way he folded his hand over hers that conveyed the need lacking in his tone. He was asking for an explanation of something he didn't understand, yet she wasn't the one to provide the answers. Even if she had the confidence to offer her opinion, which she definitely did not, he probably wouldn't like what she said. All she could do was hope that what had happened to her was beginning to happen to him—that the thing Adam was fighting so desperately just might be love.

It was that budding hope that kept her from feeling disappointment a few minutes later. After walking Stephanie to her door, Adam had waited just long enough for her to step inside before heading back to his car. Since she'd known what his answer would be, she hadn't asked him to come in.

Nuzzling Zeus as she walked down the hall to her bedroom, a slow smile crept over her face. There'd been something in the way he'd said, "See you tomorrow, sweetheart," when he'd brushed her cheek with his finger, that was making her feel rather giddy.

"Tomorrow," she whispered to the tiny dog in her arms. "I think tomorrow's going to be a wonderful day."

That prediction missed by miles.

Eight

Her alarm wouldn't stop ringing. Taking another swat at the clock, Stephanie pulled her head from under the sheet, only to realize that the racket was coming from the telephone.

"Lo," she answered, trying not to yawn.

"Ms. Moore? Nevin Dusky of the *Times*. Is it true that Dr. Adam Colter is excavating the remains of a unicorn from your property?"

Caught in midstretch, she sat bolt upright. She was about to ask the staccato-voiced man to repeat the question she was certain she couldn't have heard correctly, when the noise of the car doors slamming in front of her house split the early morning quiet. Muffled voices joined the shotlike sounds.

"Just a minute," she said into the receiver, and stumbled from her bed. Throwing back the ivory curtains covering the window, she immediately jerked them closed again. "Oh, my God," she moaned, and grabbed the filmy, hip-length robe matching the pale blue teddy she'd slept in just as the doorbell peeled for the second time.

It wasn't cars she'd heard. It was vans. Television vans. And there were cameras and cables and people swarming over her front lawn. One of those people, probably the blond woman in the business suit, was leaning on the doorbell.

The telephone!

Zeus had jumped from his basket and charged for the front door. If he'd been in it, Stephanie would have knocked him out when she nearly tripped over his new bed. "I'll call you back," she mumbled to her caller. Not knowing what else to do, she tried to break the connection so she could call Adam. The joker on the other end of the line wouldn't hang up.

Throwing the receiver onto her pillow, she started for the door. Two steps later she was turning around and heading for her closet. From what she'd heard about reporters, those cameras could very well be rolling when she opened the door, and she wasn't about to treat the world to a shot of herself looking like a *Playboy* centerfold. That was definitely not the image the principal of her school wanted his counselors to convey.

A white terry-cloth shift was jerked over her head. Swearing sharply as she pulled the brush through her sleep-tangled hair, she gave up after three strokes and flipped the brush onto the bed next to the telephone receiver. Not even breaking stride as she hurried into the living room, she scooped Zeus up as he darted toward her.

His excited yip provided the greeting when she opened the door.

"Stephanie Moore?" the woman in the suit inquired with a professional smile. The smile was suddenly gone, along with the woman's face, and Stephanie found herself blinking at the dispassionate eye of a camera. Blinking back at her was a little red light just below a KYJJ logo. "Would you care to tell our viewers..."

The strident voice of Eleanor Dobbs pierced through the smoothly delivered lead-in. "I knew it. I just knew it."

Motioning for the man with the camera to aim for the plump little woman in the flower-print dress, the reporter started down the steps. "Knew what, ma'am," she inquired as Eleanor stopped to let another camera pass. That one was on the shoulder of a man wearing a KXTV T-shirt. There was a guy behind him checking his already perfect hair in the side mirror of one of the vans.

Eleanor gave an indignant sniff. "Why, I knew that thing wasn't what they said it was. It's all just a cover-up, you know."

The newswoman clearly thought she was on to something. "A cover-up?"

Stephanie let her glance slide past the two women. She knew Eleanor and was quite certain that whatever it was the woman was thinking would never make it on the six-o'clock news.

Her eyes settled on the urbane-looking gentleman with the perfect hair. He'd stopped following the guy in the KXTV T-shirt and was apparently experiencing a very brief moment of indecision. He paused long enough to hear Eleanor say something about the remains having been identified as a man named Dino, who everyone knew was really Dean Martin, before his aggressive strides continued carrying him toward Stephanie.

She recognized him the instant he looked up at her. Brian Bain. KXTV's troubleshooter. If there was a fraud in town, that man would find it, sooner or later. Having seen him in action, she knew her best defense would have to be a good offense. The last thing he would expect was cooperation. Adam might not like the tactic she chose, but then he wasn't going to like any of this anyway.

Understating Adam's reaction was the only way she could keep herself from indulging in mild hysteria—which would be a fairly normal thing to do when a person knew they would soon be facing the wrath of Apollo. That thought made the smile she managed to plaster on her face feel rather stiff.

"Mr. Bain," she said, extending her free hand while she hugged Zeus a little tighter with the other. "How nice to meet you. I can't begin to tell you how much I admire the way you handled that bait-and-switch scam you uncovered last week."

The tactic worked. Something like shock replaced the cynical gleam in his eyes. Accepting her brisk, business-like handshake, he offered a mumbled thank-you and looked like he was about to recover from her unexpected greeting when she hit him with another technique. An appeal for help.

"Brian," she began, lowering her voice. "You don't mind if I call you Brian do you?" Not waiting for a response, she tossed a quick glance toward the crowd of neighbors gathering on her sidewalk and stifled a groan. "Cameras make me nervous. I mean, even when my dad would make home movies when I was a little girl, I'd just freeze. Couldn't move. Couldn't talk. Nothing. I'd love to talk to you, but I don't think I can with . . ."

"Hey, Bain. I got here first," the blond woman called from across the yard. Obviously disgusted with Eleanor's false lead, she tromped toward the walkway, her high heels sinking in the dew-heavy lawn.

"You only beat me by a car length, Colleen. She's talking to me."

Ignoring her competitor, Colleen planted herself on the bottom step. Her camera man followed. "Ms. Moore," she began, "Professor Mitchell said you're one of his most enthusiastic students, and he was certain you'd cooperate on this story. I've already got his interview, and all I need now are a few comments from you about how the unicorn was discovered and some footage of the unicorn itself."

Swallowing the lump of anxiety building in her throat, Stephanie hugged her curiously silent puppy even closer to her chest. Brian was blocking her from the eye of the camera. "Whatever it is that Dr. Colter is excavating hasn't been identified yet. Since it's all covered up with plastic, you..."

"You're denying Professor Mitchell's allegation then?"

Brian turned around, exposing her to the little red light. "*Are* you denying it?" he queried, motioning to his own crew.

So much for appealing to his protective instincts. Giving both reporters a polite smile, she reached behind her to open the door. "Since I'm not an expert, I'm hardly in a position to admit or deny anything. Please excuse me. I need to, ah, turn the water off in the bathtub."

Both reporters started to speak at once. But all Stephanie heard before she slammed the door behind her was Colleen's insistant, "I'm not leaving without footage!"

"Oh, Zeus," Stephanie moaned, "what am I going to do? Adam's going to kill me when he finds out about this."

Adam already knew. Signing the traffic ticket the motorcycle cop shoved under his nose, he handed the clipboard back without saying a word and pulled out onto the street. He should have known better than to ask himself what else could possibly go wrong today.

Two blocks later, he was still cursing himself, only audibly now. The string of expletives was interspersed with colorful descriptions of newspeople in general when he saw half the neighborhood crowded around the television vans.

For one irrational moment, he thought about parking his car in Linda's driveway and making a mad dash for Stephanie's back gate. Practicality immediately intervened. There was no way he'd make it past those reporters—not if they were half as tenacious as the newspaper people who'd been hounding him since six o'clock this morning. It would be better to give them a quick statement so they'd leave. No sense having what he was going to do to Stephanie on film.

"That's him!" someone shouted the instant he was out of his car. Ten seconds later, Adam was staring at microphones.

Stephanie was staring at Adam. Though he was surrounded by a contingent of her curious neighbors, she could see him quite clearly from her living room window. He seemed to be talking easily and smiling—smiling?—at the questions being thrown at him by Brian and Colleen.

A puzzled frown furrowed her brow. He didn't act upset. If anything, he seemed as comfortable as she would have guessed him to be in a classroom. He was deftly fielding the questions Brian was hurling at him by giving his answers to a suddenly very coy-looking Colleen.

The morning sun shot streaks of silver through his thick hair when he turned toward the camera the female reporter had just indicated. Stephanie could have sworn Colleen was staring at his dimple when she stepped to his side to get in the picture. Brian and his crew were already heading to their van. It wasn't until those people had moved and Adam crossed his arms that she saw how tightly his fists were clenched.

Putting Zeus into his playpen, Stephanie hurried to her room. She didn't know how long she had before she'd have to face him, but she had to do something in the meantime. Standing there waiting for the guillotine to fall wasn't doing her nerves any good.

As it was, she barely had enough time to wash her face and comb the rest of the knots out of her hair before the dreaded knock sounded. Feeling a fair amount of trepidation, she took a deep breath and, placing her hand over her throat, slowly opened the front door.

Adam's eyes, blazing with quiet fury, darted straight to her neck. "You're right to try and protect it, Stephanie. I'm not sure whose I want to wring first. Yours or that idiotic professor's."

She didn't remember moving back, but she must have. Adam had stepped inside and was closing the door with a deadly quiet click. The next backward step she took was quite deliberate.

"Are you all right?" he asked, the incisive edge in his voice making the question quite incongruous. "Did those reporters hassle you?"

Facing those reporters had been nothing compared to this. Seeing his anger fighting concern was turning her trepidation into guilt. "No. Yes. I mean, no they didn't hassle me and . . . Adam, I'm so sor—"

"I need to use your phone," he cut in, glowering down at her.

Her hand slipped farther up on her throat. He clearly didn't want her apology—and what he did want was something she didn't care to think about. There was so much coiled tension in his body that Stephanie could have sworn she saw his fingers flex as he moved toward her. His menacing step carried him right past her, though, and she slowly released the breath she'd been holding.

"What's the matter with this damn thing?" she heard him yell from the kitchen. "You got a receiver off the hook somewhere?" A very succinct expletive preceded his bellowed, "It's no wonder I couldn't get ahold of you!"

"Oh, Lord," she gasped, racing down the hall. "I forgot."

The second she picked up the receiver from her pillow she heard the high-pitched whine that had greeted Adam. That sound was irritating enough when a person was in a normal frame of mind. The sirenlike shriek had probably sent Adam, in his present state, right through the roof.

"It's okay, now," she called.

Cautiously heading out into the hall, she heard his tightly controlled request to speak with a Dr. Lebowitz. At least he hadn't gotten a busy signal.

When she entered the kitchen, Adam was sitting at the table, his elbows resting on his knees and his head bent while he listened to whatever was being said on the other end of the line. Stephanie ducked under the phone cord and walked over to the sink. Thinking that coffee might lend an air of civility to the approaching confrontation, she quietly went about filling the pot—and listened very carefully to the half of the conversation she could hear.

"I only told them that we did have a specimen under study," Adam was saying, "but that the evidence is pointing to something well within known scientific boundaries. I know it was just double-talk, Hank, but how in the hell am I supposed to tell them what it is when I don't even know? That nutty professor what's-his-name is the one you should be talking to." He paused and combed his fingers through his hair. "I know that. I'm here now. No. The reporters said she basically gave them a 'no comment.' Yes, sir, that is a relief."

The silences interspersing Adam's comments had been fairly short. The one now taking place stretched out for nearly a full minute. Watching him from the corner of her eye, Stephanie suppressed an apprehensive shiver when she heard his tight, "I realize that, sir," then cringed when she saw the way his jaw tightened.

When he lifted himself from the chair after a perfunctory goodbye, she turned toward the cabinet. If she shoved a cup of coffee into his hands, her neck should be fairly safe.

"Dammit," he seethed, slamming the phone down on its hook with such force that Stephanie nearly dropped the cups she'd just grabbed.

It would have been pure folly to ask him what was wrong. The inquiry wasn't necessary anyway. Adam was preparing to tell her in no uncertain terms as he paced the length of the counter.

It wasn't enough that he'd had to put up with her curious neighbors, her dog and the distraction of trying to work when all he really wanted to do was make love to the woman who was quietly driving him out of his mind. Now he had a whole other mess of problems. Until Stephanie came into his life he hadn't had any—none that couldn't be solved logically anyway.

"This is all I need," he said, throwing his hands in the air. "An hour ago, I thought the worst that could happen was that I'd have to cancel my class and spend the day trying to straighten out an overzealous professor and his friend at the newspaper. Now I find out that the story is damn near national news, and if I didn't already have tenure, my boss would gladly fire me! As it is, I'm not sure he won't try to find a way anyhow!"

Feeling like she'd just opened the lid on Pandora's Box, Stephanie shrank away from the angry words being hurled toward her. All kinds of horrible things seemed to be coming from that one innocuous conversation she'd had with Linda. "Adam," she began, but he wasn't listening.

"This isn't the kind of thing a pure scientist wants to be associated with, Stephanie. We go out of our way to avoid this kind of publicity. Do you have any idea what this will do to my reputation? Dr. Henry Lebowitz is probably one of the most respected men in the country." His voice grew louder as he pointed to his chest. "He's also the man I have to account to, because everything I do under the auspices of the Paleontology Department reflects on him, and now he's yelling about his department having lost all credibility because I've gotten us involved in a three-ring circus!"

A full two seconds passed while Adam replenished his oxygen supply. "I tried my damnedest to be fair with that loony mythology professor, but do you think he tried to return the favor? Hell, no! If anything, he went out of his way to make the biggest mess he possibly could. Do you know why he went to the press?"

Certain that he was about to tell her whether or not she responded, Stephanie remained glued to her spot by the sink. There was no way to stop a volcano once it began to erupt. But even an exploding Olympus would have to run out of steam eventually. In the meantime all she could do was watch in awed silence while the sparks flew and hope that the singeing fire of his wrath didn't reduce her to ashes.

"Because he didn't trust me to 'treat this with the importance it deserved,'" Adam hissed. "I gave him my word, dammit. My word! He didn't even have the decency..." The heavy slashes of his eyebrows snapped together as she swept past him. "Where are you going?"

"To change."

"I'm not finished yelling at you yet!"

"Then finish while I'm changing my clothes." Even a thundering Apollo couldn't deter her right now. Whether Adam knew it or not, she'd seen the damaged pride lying beneath his anger, and she wasn't about to let anyone get away with impugning his integrity. She'd also noticed that he hadn't gotten around to stating the obvious, but she wasn't above placing the blame where it lay. "This is all my fault," she said, hurrying into her bedroom. "So it's up to me to straighten it out."

Adam was right behind her, his footsteps as furious as his tone. "What do you think you're going to do?"

"First," she said, yanking open her closet door, "I'm going to give Professor Mitchell a piece of my mind. He may know his mythology, but he's got a thing or two to learn about professional courtesy." A beige cotton skirt was pulled from its hanger. It landed on the bed. "Then,

I'm going to talk to that boss of yours and tell him that his attitude about this whole thing stinks."

"You can't do that!"

"Oh, yes, I can. He should be standing behind you instead of demanding that you take care of this by yourself. How dare he threaten to fire you for something that isn't even your fault? It's not like you wanted any of this to happen, you know."

"Stephanie," she heard him begin just as she jerked the white terry-cloth shift over her head. The fabric covering her ears seemed to make his voice sound a little less forceful. Either that, or he'd lowered his tone. "It won't help."

"It can't hurt!" Her shift fell in a heap by her unmade bed. So did the filmy nothing of a short robe she hadn't bothered to take off before. Wearing only the ice blue teddy, she grabbed a blouse from a hanger. "As much as I love you, do you think I can just sit by and watch them make mincemeat of your reputation? We're talking about your job here, and that's not something I'm about to jeopardize any further than I already have. I'll be calm and cool and very rational. I'll tell your Dr. Leobold—"

"Liebowitz."

"Liebowitz...that I was the one who thought it was a unicorn and how you maintained a perfectly exemplary approach to the entire matter. I'll tell him it was my own stubborn refusal to listen to you and my insensitivity to your convictions that caused me to say something I should have just kept to myself."

"It won't help," he repeated.

"Why not?"

"Because I already told him that."

Stephanie was trying very hard not to think about the way Adam was so deliberately ignoring the admission that had slipped out so unexpectedly only moments ago. She hadn't meant to tell him she loved him. Not yet anyway—and certainly not in the middle of an argument. But she had, and Adam hadn't even blinked.

She was so busy trying to act like it didn't matter that she couldn't even manage indignation over what he'd said to his boss. "Maybe it will help if I confirm what you told him then," she rushed on. "Would you move please? I need to get into that drawer."

"You're not going anywhere." Curving his hand over her bare arm, he took the blouse she had clenched in her fist and laid it on the polished surface behind him. "I want you to calm down and listen to me."

It wasn't until he touched her that she noticed how much of his anger had dissipated. It was also about then that she saw the way his eyes had narrowed on the strip of skin exposed by the vee of delicate lace, and she realized what she'd been doing. In her haste to right the wrong she'd made him suffer, she'd practically stripped in front of him. The problem with impulsive decisions, she decided, was that they didn't allow time for strategic planning. He probably thought she was crazy.

She's incredible, Adam decreed to himself. All that determination and fire. And all for me.

Slowly he pulled his gaze from the agitated rise and fall of her breasts. The indignation she'd felt toward her professor, the guilt she was laying on herself, even the fierce protectiveness she was prepared to exhibit was all there in her brilliant ebony eyes. There was something else there, too. Was that the love she'd spoken of so easily? Was that the thing softening her lips into a breathless part and giving her face an almost ethereal quality?

Or was this love a combination of everything he was seeing?

"There isn't anything you can do to change what's happened," he said quietly. "We'll just let things ride for a while. Dino's identity can't remain a mystery forever and, once all the pieces fall into place, we'll know what we have. The answers always reveal themselves sooner or later."

"But what about your job?"

"Let me worry about that."

"I can't, Adam. If it wasn't for me..."

"If it wasn't for you," he interrupted, leaning against the dresser, "I'd be in a classroom right now, putting thirty students to sleep with a lecture on carbon dating, instead of standing here getting ready to take a very sexy little scrap of nothing off the woman I sometimes think has become my Nemesis. The circumstances intervening to make that possible don't really matter to me at the moment."

Before she could wonder at how he was dismissing what had happened, or decide whether or not she liked the way he'd just announced his intention, he was pulling her between his legs.

Fitting her to the insides of his thighs, he held her there with his hands loosely grasping her waist. A moment ago the fabric at her sides had felt almost cool. Now, the heat of his hands seemed to flow through the silky threads, sending a frission through every inch of skin they covered.

That rather electric sensation made it difficult to remember why she was feeling so wary. She hadn't quite forgotten, though. "Why your Nemesis?" she asked, wondering if he understood his meaning. Nemesis was the goddess of retributive justice.

"Because of who she is," he said, confirming that he did understand, "and because of what's been happening to me. I'm not talking about this little fiasco with your professor, either. Although," he added dryly, "this morning's events could certainly be considered retribution for my scientific snobbery."

A note of tempered accusation entered his deep voice. "I was quite complacent about my life until I met you, Stephanie." One tiny strap was slipped from her shoulder. "Everything fit into neat little categories, and I never allowed anyone or anything to upset the niches I created. I guess you could say I was even smug about my own inflexibility." The tip of his finger traced over her collarbone, halting when it came to the other strap. "In a way, you became my opponent. You challenged reason with the same insistence I used to defend it, and I've come away feeling more uncertain than I ever have in my life." Lifting her wrist, he bent her elbow to slip the other strap down her arm.

"I don't like not being able to understand something," he continued, watching the top of her teddy slide lower on her breasts. The silk clung precipitously to the tight pink nipples peeking through the delicate blue lace. "And I don't understand why I'm letting you make me do something I probably shouldn't."

She didn't know if it was the words themselves, or the way he was lifting the weight of her breast in his palm that was making it so difficult to comprehend what he was saying. "What are you talking about?" A tight little gasp snagged in her throat when his thumb brushed the lace over her nipple. "What shouldn't you do?"

The hand at her waist moved to her back, pressing her forward. "This," he said, dropping little nipping kisses at the corner of her mouth. "And this," he added, squeezing the soft flesh filling his palm.

A strangled "Why?" caught itself in her throat when his fingers splayed wider over her fullness.

His tongue flicked along the breathless part of her lips. "Because the more you give me, the more I'm afraid I'll want."

"Is that so terrible?"

"It is when a person isn't sure what it is they're after...or when they feel they aren't being given a choice."

The step backward she took was only mental. Adam had actually pulled her tighter against him. "You always have a choice, Adam," she said on a whisper. "I'm not forcing you to make love to me."

"Yes, you are." He smiled against her lips. "It's the only thing I can think of doing that will keep you from making a fool of yourself with my boss."

The protest she was about to utter was silenced by his mouth closing firmly over hers. He pressed his hips forward in a bold announcement of need, mimicking that erotic motion with the thrust of his tongue.

With that devastating assault on her senses, he'd just managed to erase the confusion of thoughts she'd been desperately trying to untangle. Gone was the bewilderment over his abrupt turn from anger to introspection. Missing was the dull ache that had centered in her chest when he'd failed to acknowledge her admission of love. She really hadn't expected him to return her declaration. After all, emotions weren't logical. But then, neither was the fierce possessiveness he was exhibiting now. He was touching her as if she belonged to him—as if he had every right to discover everything there was to know about her.

His hands were sure and steady when he set her away from him and pushed her teddy over her hips. That same

decisiveness revealed itself in the swiftness of his move-
ments when he tugged his red polo shirt from his jeans
and pulled it over his head. His eyes were fixed on her
face. Hers were on his fingers as he deftly unbuckled his
belt and flipped back the snap.

Raising her head when he suddenly stopped, she saw
his mouth curve in a sensual smile. "Do it for me?" he
asked.

Her throat had gone dry. Swallowing, she gave him a
little nod. Her hand was shaking when she took the metal
tab between her thumb and index finger and started to
pull it down. His hand closed over hers, pressing her
palm against him.

The warmth of his breath caressed her ear when he
flicked her lobe with his tongue. "That's right, sweetheart. Touch me the way I touch you. Make me understand."

Beneath that husky command lay a wealth of feeling
she could scarcely believe he was expressing. He was
asking for more than the physical pleasure of her caress.
He was asking her to help him admit the existence of an
emotion he was just beginning to discover. "I will," she
sighed, tasting the warm skin of his neck. Increasing the
pressure of her hand, she moved her lips along the rough
line of his jaw. "I will," she repeated, and heard him
drag in a shuddering breath.

Tactile sensations merged with less definable ones. The
friction of the well-worn denim on her palm created an
external heat that transferred itself inward, that warm
tingling centering itself deep inside her. His scent, that
heady blend of soap and musk, filled her lungs, transmitting the very essence of him to her every pore. Each
passing second made her more a part of him. Even the

pounding of her heart matched the cadence of his when her fingers splayed over the muscles banding his chest.

That erratic beat increased as she drew her tongue over one flat nipple and, slipping her hands down his sides, she eased his jeans over his hips. Following the line of curling, golden hair tapering over his stomach, she pressed warm little kisses to the tensed muscles of his abdomen, then pulled back to kneel before him while she tossed his jeans and shorts aside.

His hands closed over her shoulders, his thickened voice seeming to come from a long way off. "What are you doing, Stephanie?"

"Touching you," she said, running her hands up his legs to his hips. Her lips followed.

Bending forward, his hand curved around the back of her neck, catching a handful of her hair. When he pulled her head back, the passion tightening his features found its counterpart in her eyes. "It'll all be over in about ten seconds if you keep that up."

Her smile was partly mischief, but mostly pure feminine sensuality. "You told me to touch you."

Catching her under her arms, he lifted her to her feet. "Don't make it sound like you always do what you're told." Three steps later, he was pulling her down onto her unmade bed. "You only do what you want to do, and I think you take great pleasure in driving me crazy."

He could have been talking about her physical effect on him. Or, her inherent power to confuse his terribly rational mind. Whichever it was, she didn't waste any time trying to figure out. His body had just covered hers.

Wedging his leg between hers, he pinned her with the most consuming kiss she'd ever known. Everything he couldn't seem to say was there in the gently demanding persuasion of his mouth. It was there, too, in the bold caress of his hand massaging her breast before flattening to roam over her stomach. She belonged to him, and he knew it.

Rather than feeling threatened by his knowledge, Stephanie gloried in it. He didn't have to say the words for her to sense the depth of feeling she could see in his eyes when he gazed down at her flushed face. Just to know he needed her was enough for now. This was Adam. Real. Mortal. Not some god who only existed in imagination. Adam was a man. A man who couldn't seem to get enough of her, to get close enough to fill the need escalating between them. There was only one way to assuage that need, yet he was denying them both that fulfillment. He continued stroking her, teasing her with his kisses, until she thought she'd die from wanting.

"Open your eyes." The words came from above her, soft and distant. His weight shifted fully over her, his leg nudging hers farther apart.

The languorous desire filling her body made her eyelids feel heavy. But she complied with the quiet command. A moment later his hand pushed beneath her hips and he thrust forward. Her breath caught.

So did Adam's. Sheathed in her warmth, he could barely control the urgent demand of his body to seek completion. But he didn't want to move. Not yet. He wanted to see the play of emotions his possession had brought to her beautiful eyes; to know what it was that made him desire her like he'd desired no other.

The feel of her was too much, though. Her mouth reached up to claim his, and he found himself crushed against her, encouraging the arching of her body with the rhythm of his own, urging her ever closer to the edge of reality. He seemed to hover there, the escalating tension building until, in a spiral of untangling nerves, he felt her body flex with that same implosion of sensation. For that one, mind-distorting second they'd been hurled apart, only to come back together with a force that fused them into one irrevocable whole. The intensity of that collision seemed to release something within him he never knew existed. He wasn't at all sure what it was, but for the first time in his life, he felt absolutely complete—and, as he willed his breathing to slow, more scared than he'd ever dreamed possible.

Lifting himself to his elbows, he blinked down at the slender woman smiling up at him. "It worked," she said, sifting his hair through her fingers.

"What did?"

"You kept me from making a fool of myself with your boss. I've been thinking about it, and you're absolutely right. Telling him I think he's a jerk wouldn't help the situation any."

Trailing his finger over her kiss-swollen lips, he frowned. "I'm glad I'm right about something, but I don't think I like what you're implying. We just made love, and the only time you could possibly have thought about anything was while we were doing that."

Stephanie's smile widened. Filled with a peaceful, dreamlike contentment, she chalked the defensive edge in his tone up to a slightly wounded ego. "I decided that just now," she said to him, letting her fingers drift over his back. She'd also decided that maybe having a few differences wasn't such a bad thing after all. Adam's sensible approach might be just the anchor she needed to curb her impulsiveness. It had certainly prevented her from compounding their present problem.

Her admission was rewarded with the brush of his lips against her temple as he rolled away—and the shrill summons of the telephone.

It was Dave.

Nine

The mental picture Stephanie had concocted of D
David Abrahms bore no resemblance whatsoever to t
man himself. Having spoken with him on the phone r
less than a dozen times, she'd envisioned a rather imp
tient, scholarly and definitely older man. When he i
troduced himself from her doorstep an hour after he
called Adam, eccentric was the word that popped into h
head.

Gaping was not polite, so she tried to cover her su
prise with a smile. "Please," she said, unable to keep h
eyes from wandering the length of his slim, six-fo
frame. "Come in."

From beneath his heavy, silver eyebrows, intellige
hazel eyes stared back at her from a deeply tanned fac
Noting her less than subtle perusal, he justified his a
pearance without apology. "I was working with one
my horses when I got Adam's message to call."

That explained the disreputable jeans and dusty, lizard-skin cowboy boots. It did not, however, seem to have any connection with the impeccably tailored white shirt, the burgundy silk handkerchief and row of gold pens tucked into his pocket, or the chopper-type motorcycle he'd ridden in on. At least she could understand why his thick, silver hair looked like it hadn't seen a comb recently. Among all his other incongruities, having pure white hair at his age—somewhere around forty, she guessed—also seemed rather unusual.

"Horses?"

"I raise them. The income finances my hobby."

He'd probably think she had the intelligence of a mynah bird if she kept parroting him, but her curiosity about the man whose opinions Adam valued so highly was getting the better of her. "Your hobby?"

"Paleontology," he returned absently. "Is Adam here?"

It was apparent that Dave didn't want to stand there chatting with her. He was wearing that vague look of preoccupation she'd seen on Adam so often. "He's out back. You can come this way."

Leading him through the kitchen, she opened the back door. Expecting nothing more than a clipped thank-you, she stepped back.

Dave stopped right in front of her. "Something wrong with that dog in there?"

Realizing that he must have seen Zeus in his playpen, she shook her head. "That's the only way I can keep him from getting into trouble."

"I see," he said, then started to smile just as Adam's voice cut across the yard.

"Did you get hold of Baker?" he called from the shallow end of the hole.

Dave didn't seem to notice the absence of a greeting. Giving Stephanie a distracted nod, he crossed the patio, stepped between two three-foot hills of dirt and started for the plank. "Got him. Got Ted Sterling from up in Sacramento, too. Ted's catching the first flight out, and Baker should be here with my truck and forklift by mid afternoon. Would have brought it myself, but they're unloading hay, and we don't need 'em yet anyway." Hands on his hips, he quickly surveyed the excavation below him. "This is in better shape than I thought. Where do you want me to start?"

Whatever it was that Adam said was lost to her. Closing the door to lean against it, Stephanie tried to attribute her growing feeling of unease to those feelings of panic she'd never quite mastered, rather than to her usually reliable intuition.

Ever since Dave's call had shattered the intimacy following their lovemaking, Adam had seemed to have only one thought on his mind—getting Dino out of that hole. She knew it was important that the remains be identified as quickly as possible, especially now that the press was interested. Dave's call had obviously reminded him of that. It even stood to reason that Adam's preoccupation with the logistics of a hurried excavation might make him a little edgy. Why then, did she have the feeling that his turn from tender lover to emotionally distant scientist had started before the phone had rung?

"Oh!"

She'd still been leaning against the door. When it opened, the knob hit her in the hip. When her head snapped back, it hit wood. Propelled forward, she jerked around to face Adam's less than pleasant expression.

"What the...?" Watching Stephanie rub her head, Adam's scowl deepened. Irritation vied with concern.

That combination was becoming rather familiar. "What were you doing there? Are you all right?"

"Standing," she returned, answering his first question. "Yes," she responded to the second.

"Let me see." Pushing her hand aside, he peered down at the spot she'd been massaging. "The skin isn't broken."

With her head bent, all she could see was the enticing line of golden brown hair tapering down his chest to the low waistband of his jeans. His shirt was still in her bedroom. "I didn't think it was," she said to the buckle of his belt.

If he'd been acting a little less abrupt, she might have curved her arms around his waist. As it was, there was nothing in his manner at the moment to encourage that liberty. He'd just stepped back, his eyes cool and dispassionate.

The feeling she'd been trying to fight intensified.

"I didn't mean to come barging in like that. I should have knocked."

"You stopped knocking quite a while ago," she reminded him, hoping her smile would be returned.

It wasn't. "I guess I'd better start again. Do you have a hose we could use?"

Giving him a nod, she turned toward the laundry room door. If the strange ache filling her chest was visible in her eyes, she didn't want him to see it. It was such a dumb thing to get upset about, but she didn't want him to return to the formality of knocking before he came in the back door. She liked it when he came and went as he pleased. It made her feel as if he belonged here.

She heard him behind her as she entered the tiny room. Just as she started to open the door leading to the ga-

rage, the impatience in his voice stopped her. "I'll get it
Just tell me where it is."

"I think it's rolled up next to the rakes. If it isn't, the
I left it hooked up to the faucet out front." Her hand fe
from the knob. Turning, she found his large fram
blocking her exit. "Help yourself to anything else yo
need."

She knew there was an edge in her voice. She coul
hear it, probably better than Adam could. Somethin
inside was telling her to start backing away, to garner de
fenses against the unavoidable. The stillness in his eyes
the pinched line of his mouth, reinforced that necessity

She wasn't sure, but it sounded like he muttered, "
wish I could," as he walked out the door.

If that was what he'd said, then...

That thought was immediately curbed. She'd alread
spent the past hour trying to figure out what was goin
on, and each conclusion she'd drawn had only left he
more confused. Not knowing if she'd been coming u
with reasons or excuses for his disconcerting behavio
she canceled any further attempt at analysis. She'd leav
logic to those who could handle it. When she tried t
figure things out she never got answers. All she ever go
was a headache.

Pulling her mauve-and-white striped top over the hip
of her white slacks, she then took Zeus's leash from th
hook on the laundry room door. That poor puppy wa
spending entirely too much time cooped up, and she'
probably drive herself crazy if she didn't do something t
get her mind off Adam. She'd let Zeus take her for
walk.

"I'll be back later," she called into the garage. "D
you want the phone off the hook or on?"

Keeping her eyes on the thin strip of leather she was coiling around her finger, she waited for Adam's reply. It came in the form of a question from somewhere on the other side of her gardening supplies. "Where are you going?"

Out of my mind, she drawled to herself. "Down to the park," she told him. Her voice softened. "I won't be gone long."

Seconds after he said, "Leave it on," he heard the door shut with a quiet click. "Dammit, Stephanie," he muttered to himself. "How could I let you screw everything up like this?"

He wasn't thinking about the mess she'd helped create because of her decidedly unscientific opinions. He was thinking more in terms of his life. She'd turned it upside down, and the resulting loss of equilibrium was what he was still pondering twenty minutes later.

Dave hunkered down beside him. "It's an eye orbit, Adam, not a crystal ball. Even if it was, you won't find the answer there."

The furrows in Adam's brow deepened as he glanced up from the fragment. "What?"

Dave chuckled. "Forget it, man. You've got it bad." A knowing wink cut off the gleam in his eyes. In all the years Adam had known him, he'd never seen that look before.

The inerrant expression he was more familiar with returned to Dave's strong features. "That orbit's picked up the same coloration as the tip of the horn. First opinion would be iron oxide."

Refusing to ponder the "it" his mentor had alluded to, Adam turned away to brush the dirt from the newly uncovered fragments. "Agreed. The initial tests I ran showed there's plenty of it in this layer of soil. The black's from the tar.''

Except for the small area they were working in, the excavation was complete. All that remained was final documentation and removal. Having to work alone between classes, the task could easily take three weeks. With the help that would be arriving shortly—the professional team that had worked together on the Arizona dig—the fossil could be on its way to the lab by the day after tomorrow.

Adam wanted to think only of what he was doing—and not about the woman whose voice had coated the ragged edges of his nerves like warm honey. And, in a way, he succeeded. The thoughts running beneath the technical conversation Dave involved him in while they worked weren't about Stephanie. Not exactly. They dealt more with cause and effect.

Because of her, he'd begun to question his values, to see matters a bit differently—and to appreciate things for what they were without trying to find an explanation for their being. Only beginning to, though. He couldn't totally abandon his philosophy, and he wasn't about to try. There was still the straight and narrow of scientific logic; that rigid discipline demanding answers to unknowns. If only he could find a reasonable definition of this thing called love. Then he might know if that's what had happened to him. Had he fallen in love with Stephanie?

The lack of explanation for that much-touted phenomenon was perplexing enough. The anomaly he would have given anything to have explained to him, though, was why he was feeling so anxious, so panicked.

The person who could probably explain it to him was the last person he wanted to ask. So he asked Dave, who didn't even blink when their conversation took the abrupt

ift. His white head remained bent over the bones he
as painting with the milky solution that would protect
em from the plaster of Paris they'd be encased in later.

"Change," he replied. "We're all creatures of habit.
threat to a known form of existence has to be acknow-
dged some way, and you're acknowledging it with fear.
he male animal either reacts to fear with aggression or
ight. I'd say your fear is manifesting itself in the lat-
r."

"You sure your degree isn't in psychology, Abrahms?
hat's exactly what I feel like doing. Running."

When Dave offered him nothing but a shrug, Adam
essed on. "Anything like this ever happen to you?"

"No. Never met a lady with the right chemistry. The
es that attracted me physically didn't have any brains,
d vice versa."

"Lucky you."

The handle clattered against the side of the can when
ave dropped his brush into it and rose to his feet. With
rueful smile, he gave Adam a sideways glance. "That's
hat I try to tell myself."

By eight o'clock that evening, there was no sign that
e activity in her backyard was going to let up. Adam
asn't even going to let a setting sun deter the progress.
ghts had been strung across the hole to illuminate it.

The other two men Adam and Dave had expected had
rived within an hour of each other. A quick introduc-
n by Adam to "Ted" and "Baker," and they'd gone
aight to work. If it hadn't been necessary for the men
use her bathroom, she might not have even known they
re out there.

Needing something to do to keep herself occupied,
ephanie had fixed a huge pot of chicken and dump-

lings, which the men had consumed at the table on h
patio. Now, having gathered their empty plates and
ceived three sets of heartfelt thanks and one distract
half smile, she was once again faced with the problem
how to occupy herself. It was an odd feeling since she w
in her own home and usually found plenty to do.

By ten o'clock she'd tried watching television, wor
ing on her needlepoint and playing with Zeus. Wh
none of those activities provided any lengthy diversio
she'd given up and gone to bed with a novel. She was s
staring at the introduction when she heard Dave's Ha
ley start up a little before midnight. The wheeze of a tru
joined the roar of a Porsche engine.

Picking Zeus up from his basket, she tucked him u
der the covers with her and turned out the light.

Saturday brought more of the same, and even le
contact with Adam. Except for suggesting that she mig
want to spend the weekend with her family after all—wi
the work he had to do he obviously wouldn't be able
drive her to San Diego tomorrow—Adam had said not
ing other than a quiet thank-you for the fruit salad a
sandwiches she'd brought out. Even when she told h
she'd already called her dad to have him ship the wa
paper up, he'd said nothing. He hadn't had to. She co
tell from the way he was avoiding her eyes that he did
want her around. He couldn't very well ask her to lea
her own house, though.

One inescapable fact was becoming increasingly clea
Once Dino was gone, Adam would be, too. She or
hoped she'd have one more chance to be alone with hi
It was impossible to talk with the other men there. A
she and Adam did need to talk.

Somewhere along the line all of their differences h
ceased to matter to her. She'd discovered that what w

mportant in a relationship wasn't that the people involved shared the same interests. What mattered was that
they found each other interesting. Even though her values differed from his in some respects, Adam respected
her right to an opposing opinion as much as she did his.
That respect had probably formed the foundation of their
relationship. It had also seeded the love that had become
an irrevocable part of her being.

That kind of love didn't give up easily.

It was with that thought in mind that she led Zeus back
into the house after letting him water the hibiscus by her
front steps Sunday afternoon. What she had to do wasn't
going to be easy, and it wouldn't be long before she had
to do it.

Knowing the men were almost finished, she hurried
down the hall to the spare room. Zeus trailed after her,
nipping at her heels. The puppy stopped when she did
and cocked his head to one side.

Being an absolute sucker for that pleading look, she
picked him up and headed for the boxes of memories
stacked under the window. Kneeling on the sturdiest of
them, one full of old scrapbooks, she propped Zeus's
paws up on the frame and rubbed her chin on the soft fur
of his head. A moment later she sneezed.

Still rubbing her nose, she looked through the foot-
wide slit in the yellow curtains. The boards to replace the
section of fence her contractor had torn out when he'd
started the pool had been removed. A truck bearing the
logo of Abrahms Arabians had been backed through the
opening, and several chunks of heavy-looking white stuff
were lying on the ground beside it. A forklift was hoist-
ing a huge mass of that same substance—plaster if she
remembered what Dave had told her—onto the bed.

"That's Dino," she said to Zeus as he watched from his perch in her arms.

Adam, his voice sounding muffled through the closed window, confirmed her identification. "He's in! Let's tie him down and get him out of here."

Thirty minutes later, the forklift, the truck and everyone except Adam was gone. His back was to the house, his head bent while he stared into the gaping hole. Leaving Zeus with a dog biscuit, Stephanie slipped out the back door. Her footsteps were silent on the soft ground. The heavy, pounding noise she heard was the beat of her heart.

A tentative smile attached itself to her quiet "Hi."

Startled from whatever thoughts he'd been contemplating, Adam's head snapped up. For the briefest instant, his somber expression lightened, only to return to its former severity when his thick eyebrows knitted together.

"Hi," he returned, stepping back from the edge of the hole. Picking up the red T-shirt lying a couple of feet away, he pulled it over his head. The white lettering lined up to proclaim that "Paleontologists Do It in the Dirt."

Her glance slid to the spot where Dino—or most of him anyway—had been. "You know, it feels kind of empty out here now."

She could feel Adam's eyes traveling the length of her white jumpsuit. From the vague sensation of pressure restricting her breathing, it felt as if he was staring right through the row of yellow buttons centered between her breasts. There was nothing sensual in his inspection, though. More of a coolly calculated appraisal.

He said nothing for a moment, but she saw the muscle in his chin twitch when she turned her eyes back to his unshaven jaw. "I really appreciate everything you did, Stephanie. It was a big help."

He was referring to the meals she'd provided. A tiny shrug accompanied her quiet reply. "I like doing things for my friends."

"Is that what we are, Stephanie? Friends?"

The rapier thrust of his question was as unexpected as the challenge in his stance. Had he, too, just been waiting until there was no one around to interrupt, or overhear, what he had to say?

"I hope we are," she started, then saw a flicker of anxiety reveal itself in his narrowed eyes.

He was much better than she was at erecting defenses. But there seemed to be a very distinct crack in the armor of indifference he'd worn the past two days. Seeing that unexpected hint of vulnerability gave her the courage she wasn't sure she'd be able to find.

"I think we're a lot more than just friends. I love you, Adam."

The air surrounding them seemed to thicken. She saw his jaw harden, then a moment later his whole body seemed to relax. Slowly, his eyes made their way over her face as if committing every nuance of her expression to memory.

"I know," he whispered, touching her cheek. Then, his head was descending, his lips brushing hers in a kiss so sweetly tender it nearly brought the tears she'd refused to shed. He stepped back, leaving his thumb to caress her faintly trembling mouth. "I just wish I knew what to do about it."

Withdrawing his hand to shove it back into the pocket of his jeans, he gave her a bleak little smile.

Now. She had to do it now. "I'll tell you what you can do about it."

The wary nod he gave her was followed by an ever more reluctant, "What do you suggest?"

"That you do nothing."

"Huh?"

"It's really very simple, Adam. I'm not asking anything of you, so there's nothing for you to do." It was costing her a lot to deny herself what she wanted so badly. But she knew that the only way to hold a man like Adam was to remove the strings. "Just because I feel the way I do, doesn't mean you have to feel the same way. It's not like I'm expecting marriage and children and..."

"Children?" The way he choked the word clearly indicated that whatever thoughts he'd been entertaining, that one hadn't occurred to him.

"A mortgage," she continued, overlooking his sudden pallor. "I've already got the mortgage anyway. So you see, it's not like you have any big decision to make."

He didn't look convinced. He did, however, seem thoroughly confused. "What are you suggesting then?"

"That we just take one day at a time." Having said everything she wanted to say and feeling her courage ebb, she tried to ease off the subject. "Maybe you could even help me perfect my serve on one of those days."

To her surprise, Adam didn't take the escape she'd offered. "No changes? No commitments?"

It was impossible to interpret his bland tone. "Nothing has to change." Mentally crossing her fingers, she met his eyes as evenly as she could. "No commitments."

He didn't sound anywhere near as pleased as she'd thought he would. "Are you saying you wouldn't want to marry me?" Looking as shocked to have posed that question as she was to hear it, he quickly added, "Hypothetically speaking."

Willing her heart to move from her throat back to her rib cage, she scolded herself for jumping to conclusions. He hadn't asked her to marry him. He'd only asked if she was opposed to the idea. His expression certainly indicated that he wasn't in favor of it. More than likely, it was only a threatened male ego that had prompted the inquiry anyway. No man would like to think he'd be refused, should the offer be made.

"I didn't say that," she evaded, determined to keep her pride intact. It would hardly improve her position to tell him she'd marry him in a minute. She was trying to impress him with her lack of tenacity, not scare him off with broad hints at permanency. She didn't want to close any doors, though, either.

"You'd never make it as a poker player," he surprised her by saying. "There's too much in your eyes." As he slowly scanned her upturned face, some of his perplexity vanished. Without it, his tension was again noticeable. It was a disquiet tempered with tenderness.

"I think I understand what you're trying to do, Stephanie, but I can't compromise you like that. You may think you'd be willing to settle for less than what you want, but you'd either wind up resenting me or hating yourself. You mean too much to me to let that happen."

Not waiting to see what kind of response he'd provoked, he picked up the bundle of sticks that had formed the grid work. "I'd better go," he said. "The guys'll be waiting for me."

His face was shadowed with some thought he clearly wasn't going to share. Knowing she had nothing to gain by saying anything else, she simply watched while he adjusted the weight of the bundle and turned away.

A moment later, he glanced back over his shoulder. 'Stephanie, I . . . I need to think."

Ten

Thank God that's over." Stephanie heaved a sigh of relief. Only one more class to go, and she'd no longer have to bear Professor Mitchell's icy glares.

Linda, following her out of the Humanities Building, turned her frown to the steps they were descending. "I now know how it must feel to be invisible. Too bad I wasn't a couple of weeks ago."

A sympathetic smile was tossed over Stephanie's shoulder. When Linda had returned to class after her vacation, she'd been subjected to the same stony silence Stephanie had now borne from the professor for two weeks. He hadn't said a word to Stephanie. She hadn't said anything to him, either. Her opinion of his actions wasn't necessary anyway. The Board of Regents had already informed him of their displeasure over what she had come to think of as "the incident."

There were times when it seemed like it had never happened. The press had grown bored with the story as soon as they'd discovered there'd be no immediate answers. The last item Stephanie had seen on it had been a two-inch column buried in the back of the paper, next to the obituary page.

"Do you want to walk by the Science Building?" Linda posed the question the moment she saw Stephanie's head turn in that direction.

With a hesitant smile, she shook her head. "That would be too obvious. We have no reason to be on that end of the campus, and he knows it." Much like a tired runner facing the last mile of a race, she forced her feet to move toward the proper destination—the parking lot.

Her relationship with Adam was something else that seemed to be rapidly fading into obscurity. If it hadn't been for the memories compounding the dull ache constantly filling her, she might not have known the man even existed. Like Apollo returning to his netherworld, he'd vanished within the walls of his academic Olympus, never to be heard from by a mere mortal like her again. A very vital part of her existence had gone with him.

Linda worried the flesh of her bottom lip. "Are you sure I shouldn't talk to him?"

"I'm positive." Poor Linda. She felt so responsible. "I've told you before that what happened between Adam and me has nothing to do with what you said to Professor Mitchell. You know how analytical Adam is. I'm sure he had to weigh the pros and cons of our relationship, and in doing that he apparently decided he doesn't want me." She blinked up at one of the light standards growing out of the hedge. Why did it have to hurt so much to say that? "Everything always works out for the best . . . even if we can't always see it at the time."

How hollow that philosophy sounded to her now. Having vacillated between hurt, anger, acceptance and denial, Stephanie had tired of telling herself everything would be all right. Yet, she kept right on doing it. She had to. It was the only way she could deal with the thought of all the empty tomorrows she had to face without Adam.

This section of the parking lot was surrounded by a serpentinelike chain threading a row of low posts. Since Linda was stepping over it, she didn't see the pain in Stephanie's eyes. All she heard was the protective lightness that had been forced into her tone.

"You're really incredible, you know that? My God, Stephanie, if the man I loved had walked out two weeks ago, saying nothing more than 'I need to think,' the very least I'd do is try to find out what it was he had to think about. Does he need to think about having an affair, or having you live with him, or whether or not you should stay friends? The way he left it, you don't even know if he was really saying, 'So long, sport. It's been real.' It wasn't fair of him to leave you hanging without a clue."

Stephanie was inclined to agree, and a clue was the last thing she expected when she answered her doorbell that afternoon to find one of Adam's students standing on her front porch.

Ronald, the bespectacled half of Ronald-and-Herbert, gave her a sheepish smile. He also handed her an envelope. "It's from Dr. Colter," he said, using his index finger to push his glasses up the bridge of his nose. "Nice seeing you again, Ms. Moore."

For a full minute after Ronald left, Stephanie stood staring at the small manila envelope she was holding. Thinking she might as well sit down before the need to do so fully presented itself, she moved the needlework that

ad occupied her last night from the arm of the sofa.
itting on the freed space, she slowly extracted the neatly
olded sheet of paper as if a quicker movement might
nake it explode. Again she hesitated.

"Come on," she coached herself, knowing full well
vhy her hand was shaking. "Unfold it. The worst it can
e is a 'Dear Jane.'"

She couldn't tell what it was. Adam's writing was clear
nough. It was what he'd written that didn't make any
ense. Even when she read the cryptic note for the third
ime it failed to hold any significance.

Stephanie: I told you that nothing remains a mystery forever. The identification is positive. It's the counterpart to $E = MC^2$. $L = AS^3$.

Adam

She had no trouble recognizing Einstein's theory of
elativity. Only recognizing it, though. The theory was
eyond her comprehension; she couldn't even remember
vhat the letters stood for. And she certainly didn't un-
erstand that next equation. What did physics have to do
vith anything?

"Of course," she said with a bittersweet smile. "'The
lentification is positive.' He's talking about Dino."

Adam had known she'd be curious about Dino's iden-
ty. It was rather thoughtful of him to send someone all
ne way over to her house to let her know that the mys-
ery had been solved. Thoughtful, but a wasted effort.
he still had no idea what Dino was. If Adam thought
ne'd know from his hieroglyphics, he was definitely
iving her more credit than she deserved. She should have
pened the note before Ronald left so he could have ex-

plained it to her. As it was, Zeus had as good a shot as she did at guessing what the second equation meant.

A half an hour later, Stephanie had concluded a rather one-sided debate with the puppy who'd faithfully followed her around the living room while she finished watering her plants. Zeus had cocked his head attentively while she voiced the arguments for and against calling Adam to thank him for the note—and to have him explain, in English, just exactly what Dino had turned out to be. Zeus had blinked in agreement when she'd decided not to call. If Adam had wanted to talk to her, he would have called himself instead of sending a student with a note.

That conviction was what kept her heart from sliding to her throat when the phone rang and she answered Linda's buoyant "What's up?" with a credibly casual "Not much. I was just thinking about going to the library."

"Oh, you can't do that! Ah...I mean, can you wait for a while?"

More than a little puzzled by the sudden frantic note her friend was trying to cover, Stephanie's brow pleated. "Sure it can. Why?"

"Oh, I..." It was apparent enough that the wheels in Linda's head were whirring. It was also pretty obvious that she hadn't expected Stephanie to throw a wrench into whatever it was she wanted by taking off for the library. "I have to go out for a while...ah, it's an errand for Ed, and I'm expecting a delivery from UPS. The truck usually goes through our neighborhood around three, so if you wouldn't mind watching for it and getting the package from the driver, I'd really appreciate it. It's awfully important."

It was also awfully strange that Linda's car was still parked in her driveway an hour and a half later. Stephanie had agreed to wait for this mysterious package—the one that hadn't been delivered when the UPS truck had driven by without stopping a few minutes ago—and was now wondering if she shouldn't go next door and ask her flaky neighbor what was going on.

She was halfway out the back door when Zeus's agitated barking stopped her. Instead of following her out, he'd headed for the front door. Cutting back across the kitchen, she heard a distinct, clopping noise. It was followed by a whinny. There was no mistaking what was making those sounds. It was a horse. And the muffled snorts were coming from in front of her house.

Zeus had gone crazy—which was exactly what she thought had happened to her when she looked out the picture window. Firmly convinced that she'd lost her mind along with her heart, she closed her eyes to dispel the unbelievable sight before her.

When she opened them a second later, it was still there.

Loving Adam must have driven her off the deep end. She could swear that right there, prancing in her driveway, was a huge, white Arabian with a three-foot horn growing just beneath its forelock.

Everything about the proud animal was nothing less than magnificent—from the high arch of his long tail to the painstakingly painted horn strapped to his arrogantly held head. The horn even had a notched spiral threading its three-foot length.

Stephanie was no longer looking at the horse, though. Slipping out the door before Zeus could, she kept her eyes on the man sitting astride it. Never would she have thought Adam capable of something so outrageous. He never had quite fit the professorial clichés, but there'd

always been that underlying reserve—maybe even stu
finess—that kept him from doing the truly ridiculous.

"Adam," she said, crossing her arms over the ice-blu
T-shirt tucked into her beige shorts. Sitting up there lik
that, dressed in jeans and a bright blue shirt that faith
fully matched his eyes, he looked like a warlord who'
taken a wrong turn in a time tunnel. "Are you nuts? Yo
can't have a horse out here."

The sight of that dimple of his didn't do a thing to a
leviate the unhealthy beat of her heart. "I got a permi
Want to go for a ride? We can only go to the end of th
block, though. That's where Dave's waiting for me wit
the trailer."

The caution in her approach wasn't there because sh
feared the restless animal. It was there because she wa
afraid Adam's reason for doing this might not be the or
she so desperately needed.

"It's all right," he said, moving his foot from the sti
rup of the gleaming silver saddle. Indicating that sh
should step there, he held out his hand. "I won't let yo
get hurt."

The intense blue of his eyes bore down on her, ma
nifying his meaning. Still unwilling to let herself believ
the message she seemed to see so clearly, she slipped he
hand into his and was pulled up to sit in front of him.

"Comfortable?"

All she could do was nod. Comfort was a relative term

His thighs molded the sides of her hips. The soft deni
covering his legs moved to settle against her calves. Sh
felt the pressure of his arm curling loosely around he
waist, and his warm breath feathering the hair tumblin
against her neck. Taken individually, those sensation
were tantalizing enough. Combined, their effect wa
devastating.

She fixed her eyes on the intricately painted horn. It looked as if it was made of papier-mâché. She felt composed entirely of knotted nerves. "Why did you do this?"

"Because I wanted to give you your unicorn. Since Dino turned out to be an antelope, this is as close as I could come. We found the stub of a second horn on one of the skull fragments, but it took us awhile to identify a genus because true antelopes aren't native to this continent. The nearest we can figure is that some early travelers brought it along as a good-luck talisman." Chuckling, he shrugged, which made his chest move lightly against her back. "We can talk about this later. Ready?"

Again she nodded, not trusting herself to speak. He wanted to give her a unicorn. Those words, coming from Adam, were the most beautiful ones she'd ever heard.

The excited shouts of children, those that could be heard over Eleanor's incredulous "My God! It's real!" filled the air. When Adam reined to the left, Stephanie caught sight of Linda. Adam was giving her a thumbs-up, and Stephanie saw her friend's grin widen.

"This is why she wanted me to stay home," she said almost to herself.

"Uh-huh. There was no way I was going to bring this horse over here if you were gone."

"So you called Linda. No wonder she sounded so strange when I told her I was going to the library."

"What were you going to the library for?"

"To get a book on physics."

Adam's arm tightened around her waist as they cantered out of the driveway. The horse gave a snort and tossed his head. "Why?"

"To see if I could figure out your equation for Dino
Now that you told me what he is...or was, I know the A
stands for antelope, but . . ."

"No, it doesn't."

"It doesn't?"

Stephanie had been oblivious to the people emerging
from their front doors as the horse headed down th
palm-lined street. It was only when Adam hadn't re
sponded, and she shifted to glance around at him that sh
noticed the curious stares they were drawing. "Oh, goo
grief." Ducking her head, she tightened her grip on th
saddle horn. "We're making a spectacle of ourselves.
have to live in this neighborhood, Adam."

"So will I. If you want me. Hold still," he continue
as if he'd just remarked on the weather. "Any sudde
moves, and this guy might break into a gallop. Now, bac
to your neighbors. They're probably getting used to th
entertainment you've been providing. First there was th
police, then my crew, and we can't forget the reporters."

His throaty chuckle vibrated the length of her spine
Closing her mouth, which had fallen open a couple sec
onds ago, she glanced in the direction Adam was point
ing. Dave was leaning against the horse trailer parke
half a block away.

She barely noticed. She was too busy trying to absor
what she'd just heard. If she wanted him? That was wha
he'd said, wasn't it? "What do mean by you'll have t
live here, too?"

Adam didn't even hesitate. "Husbands and wive
usually live together, don't they? I suppose we could liv
in my apartment, but there wouldn't be a yard for Zeu
or your flowers. Of course, we could buy something to
gether, but after all the work you've put into your place

didn't think you'd want to move. When will they finish
he pool?''

Wishing that this discussion was taking place somewhere other than on the back of a horse whose owner was
ow walking toward them, she replied, "Mr. Johnson
aid they'd be here tomorrow."

Stephanie was barely aware of whatever it was Dave
aid to her or what she said to Micky and Matthew and
he other children that accompanied her and Adam back
o the house. She knew she'd smiled at the boys—she
eemed to be smiling at everything—and vaguely re-
nembered agreeing that the unicorn was "really neat."
Whatever else she'd said or done was beyond recollec-
on. Her awareness was only on the man watching her
ow from where he leaned against the arm of her sofa,
almly petting her dog.

She was still flattened against the door she'd closed a
ull thirty seconds ago. Thinking that he was waiting for
er to break the electric silence, she stifled the urge to
ush into his arms and prepared to offer him a drink in-
.ead. If he was as nervous as she was, he could prob-
bly use one. "Would you...?"

"Stephanie, I..."

Their simultaneous beginnings abruptly ended. Zeus
lled in the momentary gap, growling in disapproval
hen Adam left him draped over a mauve throw pillow.

With a hesitant smile, she moved from the door. "You
rst."

Adam, rubbing his jaw, took another step toward her.
he confidence he usually exuded was missing. In its
lace was a brand of hesitation with which he clearly
asn't comfortable. "What I said before," he began,
nly to start over again. "I tried..." That apparently
asn't the opening he wanted, either.

"Kiss me, Adam?"

The hesitation was gone. Matching the two steps h
took, she found herself in the only place she'd eve
wanted to be. In his arms. The tense line of his mout
softened against hers, lingering with hints of desire hel
in check to speak a message beyond physical need. Tha
need was there in the tender insistence of his lips, evok
ing silent promises of the passion to come. But a greate
desire had manifested itself—the necessity of being hel
by the person who means more to you than anything els
in the universe.

"I've missed you so much." Her words were muffle
against his chest as he cradled her against him.

A gentle kiss was placed on the top of her head, ar
other was pressed to her temple. "I've missed you, too.
A third touched her cheek when he nuzzled his face close
to hers. "I've missed *us*."

His tongue flicked the corner of her lip. An instar
later she was tasting the minty warm flavor of his mout
as she hungrily explored the moist interior. The har
muscles of his chest seemed to slack, his low groa
sounding like that of a starving man finally findin
sustenance. Drawing his hands up her sides, his finger
moved toward the fullness straining against him. Tha
upward movement ceased. With his hands curved aroun
her rib cage, he drew back.

"I love you, Stephanie."

The husky sound of his voice slowly filtered throug
the deafening roar in her ears. Staring up at him, sh
found those words repeating themselves in his eyes.
feeling of tightness, not unlike that of a hand squeezin
around her heart, filled her chest. She thought it migl
burst.

The words of love she'd meant to speak, those illuming her expression, remained on the tip of her tongue. Adam, smiling down at her with that sexy grin, was pulling her to him again.

"You know that note I sent you?"

Raising her head from his chest, she nodded.

With his hand on her cheek, he nudged her head back down again. "I was working in the lab last night when it finally occurred to me. The reason I was having so much trouble convincing myself that I didn't want my life to change was because it already had." He paused for a moment. "Did that make sense?"

"Uh-huh."

"Well, anyway. Once I stopped fighting that, it was easy to figure out why I felt so miserable. Half of me was missing the part that made everything else matter. That's when it hit."

Adam was stroking the back of her hair. She started to lift her head, only to find the pressure of Adam's hand preventing it. "What did?"

"The equations that made what happened to me the other morning make sense. Einstein's theory, energy equals mass times the velocity of light squared, has a counterpart."

"Was that the equation in the note?"

She felt his lips on her forehead. "The same. 'Love equals Adam and Stephanie to the third power.' I figure that love is like the energy in Einstein's theory. It isn't tangible, but it's just as real."

The man was incredible. Even now he had to have an explanation for the why of something. A contented smile curved her mouth, and she tightened her arms around him. His theory would never find its way into a scientific journal, but it had just changed her world completely.

"Why the third power?" she asked, and felt him shift against her.

He cupped her face, his smile wicked with the sensual gleam in his eyes. "That's where we need to experiment more." Trailing his finger down the vee of her blouse, he neatly flicked the button from its hole. The rest followed in quick succession.

"The third power," he whispered, nipping the tender flesh of her neck as her hands worked their way beneath his shirt, "is our child. You do want children, don't you?"

"Oh, Adam. I love you."

"Does that mean yes?"

She answered him with her kiss, sweetly tender and filled with the same yearning compelling his touch. It was impossible, but she could have sworn she heard the gods in their heavens sigh with approval.

The child Stephanie and Adam would create would have its feet planted firmly on the ground and its head in the stars. It would be born of the special love they shared that seeks not to change, but to accept and understand. A kind of love so powerful, it was the stuff of legends.